BLOOD

ON HIS HANDS

ALSO BY WILLO DAVIS ROBERTS

The Absolutely True Story

Baby-sitting is a Dangerous Job

Buddy is a Stupid Name for a Girl

Don't Hurt Laurie

Hostage

Kidnappers

Megan's Island

Nightmare

Pawns

Rebel

Scared Stiff

Sugar Isn't Everything

Twisted Summer

Undercurrents

View from the Cherry Tree

What Could Go Wrong?

BLOOD
ON HIS HANDS

WILLO DAVIS ROBERTS

Simon Pulse
New York　London　Toronto　Sydney

To Garth, one of the kids who have added joy and education to my life, in the hope that he will never experience anything like this adventure except through this book.

SIMON PULSE
An imprint of Simon & Schuster Children's Publishing Division
1230 Avenue of the Americas, New York, NY 10020
Copyright © 2004 by Willo Davis Roberts
All rights reserved, including the right of reproduction in whole or in part in any form.
SIMON PULSE and colophon are registered trademarks of
Simon & Schuster, Inc.
Also available in an Atheneum Books for Young Readers hardcover edition.
Designed by O'Lanso Gabbidon
The text of this book was set in Jenson Text.
Manufactured in the United States of America
First Simon Pulse edition January 2006
10 9 8 7 6 5 4 3 2 1
The Library of Congress has cataloged the hardcover edition as follows:
Roberts, Willo Davis.
Blood on his hands / Willo Davis Roberts.—1st ed.
p. cm.
Summary: After the death of his little sister, Marc's life begins to fall apart when his parents divorce and his mother comes under the influence of a pushy insurance agent whose dislike of Marc lands him in a camp for socially maladjusted youths.

ISBN: 978-1-4814-4461-3

[1. Family problems—Fiction. 2. Emotional problems—Fiction.
3. Grief—Fiction.] I. Title.
PZ7.R54465Bl 2004
[Fic]—dc22
2003011072

1

Somewhere in the distance, behind him, Marc heard a hound baying.

He hesitated, breathing hard, wiping the sweat off his forehead with the back of his hand, straining to hear better.

The pines rustled around him, barely audible and producing no cooling breeze at ground level in the midday sun. A jay screeched overhead and showed a flash of brilliant purplish blue.

The hound bayed again, a lonely, fearsome sound.

Had he inadvertently strayed near some isolated cabin and been overheard by a watchdog? Or had they already missed him and called in bloodhounds to track him?

He felt as if he'd been running for hours, though it couldn't have been nearly that long. The mountainside was tufted with coarse grass and unfamiliar weeds, and there were hidden holes, probably snakes' or chipmunks' or rabbit burrows. Once he'd stuck his entire foot into a large one, and his ankle still ached where he'd twisted it. He was grateful he hadn't broken it. Nobody'd ever find him out here until he'd starved to death, he thought grimly, if he couldn't walk.

Beside him, Rat whined and licked at his jean-clad knee.

"We can't rest yet, buddy," Marc told the dog. "We haven't gone far enough. As soon as they find Stoner they'll be after us."

Rat licked him again, as if he understood. Rat would be the only one who did, he thought bleakly, and blinked the moisture from his eyes, determined not to cry. If he'd made it through this far without crying like a fourteen-year-old baby, it was no time to start now.

The hound had stopped making a racket, so maybe it wasn't following his scent after all. He wasn't kidding himself that they'd never catch up with him, but at least if he could reach his dad, he'd have somebody on his side. Somebody who could maybe do something.

What did they do to juveniles in California when they're convicted of murder? He could swear it was self-defense, but who knew if anybody would believe him? Would they accept that he was protecting his dog, after Stoner had kicked him into the bushes, and that Marc had known he was next?

He hit a steeper embankment, and the rough turf gave way to shale that broke and skidded under his feet, sliding him backward. He dropped to his knees to grab hold of a scrubby bush that tore his hands.

Rat whined again, tongue hanging out, and Marc knew the dog was as thirsty as he was. If he hadn't been in such a panic, he'd have grabbed a water bottle; Stoner's was right there on the ground beside him, probably full. Lifesaving, maybe, even if it did have blood on it.

If wishes were horses, beggars would ride. Sure. If, if, if.

Painfully, he began to crawl up the slope until he regained more level ground. There were more trees here, offering a small patch of shade. Rat flopped down on his belly, panting, and Marc gave in and sprawled too.

Behind him, around him on all sides, were dark green cedars and pines that faded into misty blue in the distance. The earth itself, between the rocks, raised a red powdery dust at his touch.

Somewhere above him, he was pretty sure, was Interstate 5, snaking its way through the Siskiyous on its way through the entire length of California, through Oregon, and on up into Washington State, all the way to Seattle and beyond to the Canadian border.

Seattle, where, if he was lucky, he'd make connections with his dad.

He wished he knew if it was safe to emerge onto the freeway, and if he'd have a chance of hitching a ride. Oh, he knew hitchhiking was dangerous, but not reaching his father was even more so, wasn't it?

How soon would they get the cops to get out an all points bulletin? Would his escape from the camp be on the news yet? Or did he still have a little time? If he crossed into Oregon, would they be looking for him there?

His breathing was quieting, and Rat nosed his hand. "Yeah, I'm thirsty too," Marc murmured, stroking the soft spotted head. "Maybe up on the interstate there's a rest stop where there's water. We might even come across a little stream somewhere before then."

He didn't move, though. It felt good just to sit there

for a few minutes and try to think of the logical thing to do next.

There had been a time when he'd have prayed about it. That's what his parents and his grandmother had taught him when he was just a little kid. Pray for help when you're stuck. God's always with you, always hears you. It had been a long while since he'd felt God's presence in his life.

He no longer trusted God to make things right.

Not since they'd said all the prayers for Mallory, and she'd died anyway.

Instead of planning his strategy, he sat there and remembered.

He and his little sister had never been buddies. After all, when he was twelve, she was only six, and a girl <u>at that.</u> She didn't want to learn to throw or bat a ball, or wrestle, or read adventure books. She was into dolls and tea parties and dressing up in Mom's high heels and trailing fancy gowns on the floor.

To tell the truth, he'd hardly noticed her, most of the time. When he'd slammed the car door on her fingers, turning them purple, he'd been genuinely sorry and held ice on her hand, wrapped in a wet washcloth. When he'd been assigned the task of supervising her bath, because both Mom and Dad were busy doing something else, he'd sat on the toilet and read the latest Roland Smith or Bill Wallace adventure while Mallory splashed around in the tub until she was clean enough for him to wipe her off.

There were a few times when she'd gotten into his room and messed something up, and then he'd been annoyed with her. But when he'd scolded her for disturbing his papers, or for spilling the poster paints he'd been using on a school project, her blue eyes had filled with tears, and he hadn't been able to stay mad at her.

It was only when she got sick that Marc started thinking of her as an individual, one who suffered pain. Even then, he wasn't concerned much at first. He'd been busy doing things with his friends, adjusting to seventh grade and a new teacher, Mr. Hepner, who was a whole different ball of wax from Miss Schering and her fluttery manner. Mr. Hepner didn't put up with any nonsense of boys poking people with sharpened pencils or sticking their feet out into the aisles when anyone tried to walk by. He expected you to do your homework on time, and to be paying attention when he called on you so he didn't have to repeat himself.

But the teacher had led an interesting life, and every day he shared some of the things he'd learned, and the places he'd been. Marc was fascinated by the possibilities that lay ahead for a young guy who wanted to try a lot of different things.

He didn't pay any attention when Mom mentioned her concern about Mallory's gradual loss of energy and interest in things that had formerly kept her entertained. He heard Dad suggest taking his sister to the doctor for a checkup, but was really more interested himself in finishing up dinner and escaping for a game of sandlot softball before it got dark.

He heard Mom report that Dr. Uvaldi had ordered a bunch of lab work done, and Mallory displayed for him the bruise on her arm where they'd taken "a whole lot of blood. It hurted," she'd said.

"Bummer," Marc said, but he often had bruises and scrapes, and it didn't seem overly important.

Not until he came home one warm afternoon and met his dad, arriving home hours earlier than usual.

"You get fired?" Marc demanded jokingly, but Dad didn't laugh.

"Mom called. They got the results of Mallory's lab tests," he said. Even as self-absorbed as Marc was, he caught the hint of something serious.

"She's not really sick, is she?"

"That's what she called me home to tell me," Dad said, and strode into the house, with Marc following.

Mom's eyes met Dad's, then she licked her lips and swung her attention to Marc. "Honey, take Mallory out on the swing for a few minutes while I talk to your father," she said. Her voice quavered.

"Sure," Marc said, disappointed that he wasn't going to sit in on the family conference. "Come on, sprout, let's go swing."

Uncharacteristically, Mallory stuck out her lower lip. "I don't want to swing," she said. "It makes me feel sick."

Mom's hands clenched in her lap. "Take her for a walk then. Or read her a story."

Mallory opted for the story, and they went upstairs, where she picked out a book Mom had recently bought her. Mallory was very fond of *Hooway for Wodney Wat,* and though Marc was already tired of reading it, he resigned himself to putting up with it one more time.

It was a short book, and when he'd finished, he wasn't sure how much longer he had to keep his little sister occupied.

"I'm really tired," Mallory said. "I think I'll take a nap."

Marc looked at her sharply, and saw a child who had lost her usual color and showed bluish shadows under her eyes. Mallory never took naps.

He didn't argue, though. "Okay," he said, and left her curling up on one of her twin beds. Then he made his way down the stairs, quietly, so his parents wouldn't hear him coming.

He knew before he reached the doorway to the living room that his mother was crying.

"But it's not certain, yet, is it?" Dad was asking. "There's a chance they've made a mistake."

"The nurse wasn't supposed to have let me know; she just thought the doctor had already told me, and she was trying to be encouraging. Dr. Uvaldi was upset, because he said if there's bad news they try to always have both parents present when they tell them the prognosis."

"But he also said he wanted to repeat some of the tests, Patty. That means he wasn't satisfied with these first results," Dad said, sounding as if he was trying to convince himself as well as her. "We don't need to panic yet."

"But what if it's true? What if she really does have leukemia?" Marc's mother wailed softly, and Marc saw now that his parents were standing in an embrace in the middle of the room, each of them making an effort to hold the other up. Marc's father was a head taller than his mother.

Leukemia? Marc didn't know much about medicine; but that was a name he'd heard. It meant something awful, didn't it? He sucked in a painful breath and made his presence known.

"Leukemia? Mallory has leukemia?"

His father turned toward him, his face etched with lines that hadn't been there minutes earlier. "It's not certain yet. They have to repeat some of the tests."

"But they think she does? That's . . . People die from leukemia, don't they?" Marc asked, feeling numb, in shock. Mallory was only six. She couldn't die.

His mother, incapable of answering, collapsed in her husband's arms. He was clearly as stricken as she was. Marc had never seen either of them in the shape they were in at this moment. They'd always taken care of everything, protected their kids from any sort of peril. His entire world was rocked around him.

He'd actually considered his parents overprotective, insisting on crash helmets and shin guards and keeping them informed where he was all the time; warning him against trying drugs or getting into a car with anyone without their permission; setting curfews and requiring that they be met; knowing who his companions were and knowing their parents.

But they'd never made a rule against leukemia. What could anyone do against a hazard like that?

The Solie family had always been strong and united and happy. They lived in a decent house and drove nice cars and went to church and celebrated Christmas and Thanksgiving and Easter with great joy and enthusiasm. Marc and Mallory usually got pretty much what they asked for their birthdays, within reason. They'd hardly ever been deprived of anything they needed or truly wanted.

Marc felt his universe crumbling, his foundations unable to hold him. It couldn't be true; nobody in their family could be dying. Yet he felt as if *he* were, the strength leaking out of his legs so that he was going to fall down.

"Marc, get Mom a glass of water," his father said then, and Marc made himself move, go to the kitchen, get a glass and fill it.

Patty Solie was sitting on the couch when he got back to the living room with it, her face streaked with tears. Her husband sat beside her and held the glass for her, putting an arm around her comfortingly.

Dad would make it all right, Marc thought desperately. He always did.

Only, incredibly, he did not.

2

If anyone had told him what was going to happen to his family, Marc would have vehemently denied that it was possible.

More blood was drawn from Mallory's small arm, leaving another massive bruise, and they waited for the results. Marc knew the moment his parents walked into the house from the doctor's office that there had been no mistake: The diagnosis of leukemia was correct.

His parents tried to hold it together. They clung to each other, and his mother tried valiantly to keep from falling apart in front of him and Mallory. Of course, they would consult specialists. The doctors in Eureka encouraged them to take Mallory to San Francisco for a second opinion, and then a third.

They didn't take Marc with them, but called in his grandmother to stay with him during the four days they were gone. Grandma Belle tried to pretend that things were normal, baking him a cherry pie, making hamburgers for supper, talking in her usual cheerful manner, until Marc finally blurted across the table, "Mallory's going to die, isn't she?"

"We don't know that yet. Other doctors might have some idea what to do for her," Grandma said.

"What if they don't?" Marc pushed.

"Then we'll pray," Grandma Belle told him. "Prayer can accomplish miracles, honey."

Only in this case, it didn't. The Solies returned from San Francisco devastated. Mallory had a rare form of the disease, and though the doctors would attempt to treat her, the family had been informed that statistically there was less than a 10 percent chance of success.

They put Mallory on the prayer chain not only at their own church, where the entire congregation joined them, but at other area churches attended by anyone they knew. The newspaper ran a story about Mallory, and various organizations held fund-raising efforts, because in addition to the mounting medical bills not covered by insurance, the family expenses for travel and out-of-town accommodations needed to be covered as well.

At first Dad took time off from his job as dispatcher for a trucking firm to make the trip to the city, nearly three hundred miles to the south. But after the first month, he felt he had to go back to work, and he left Mom and Mallory at the hospital and went down only on weekends.

When he finally took Marc along, after weeks of virtually ignoring his existence to concentrate on Mallory, Marc felt like an outsider. The hospital, the nurses, the doctors, so familiar to his parents, were all strange to Marc. The hospital was so much bigger than the one back home that it made him more scared than he'd already been.

During this visit, Marc's terror had mounted to the edge of hysteria. The first time he saw his little sister, she looked so sick that he was unable to control the tears that flooded his eyes. When he approached her bed, Mallory produced a watery smile. "Hi, Marc."

"I brought you something," he said, thrusting a stuffed animal at her, a white and black striped tiger Their parents had paused in the doorway to speak to a nurse, and it was almost as if they were alone together.

"Thank you," she said, but she didn't even put out a hand to touch the soft fur. When she fixed them on his face, her eyes seemed a paler blue than he remembered. "Did they tell you I'm going to die?"

"No!" He strangled on the denial. "Everybody in town's praying for you—"

"God will be glad to see me when I get to heaven, won't He?"

His heart pounding, Marc didn't know what to say. He wanted to touch her, yet she looked so fragile that he didn't quite dare. For a moment he hated them all—the doctors, the nurses, even his parents—for not being able to do anything to stop what was happening to Mallory.

If something so terrible could happen to an innocent little girl, it could happen to him, too. It could happen to anybody.

Then Mallory stretched out a tentative finger and ran it between the ears of the stuffed tiger. "It's beautiful, Marc. Keep it when I'm gone, to remember me by."

There was no controlling the spurt of tears, though he blinked them back desperately. He wanted to deny that she would be gone, but how could he? "I'll always remember you," he said awkwardly. His agony by now unbearable, he demanded, "Did they tell you that? That you're going to die? The doctors?"

"No, but I can tell. It's all right." She moved her hand from the tiger to his hand, a touch as light as a feather, as if she were already almost gone from this life. "I'm not scared anymore, honest. When I die it won't hurt anymore, and I won't feel sick. I'm glad you came this time, Marc. I wanted them to bring you before, but they thought I looked too awful. They don't let me look in a mirror, but I know—I can see the bruises on the rest of me. I don't think I'll still be here when everybody comes again, so thank you for coming."

That was quite a mature speech for a six-year-old. Marc had no idea how to respond, and he wanted to flee from the room, from impending death, to scream out his fury and frustration. But he stood there beside the high bed, until his parents finally returned.

They reached out for Mallory, and at last Marc broke free of the family group and blindly made his way out into the corridor. He didn't know where he was going, but he had to escape this awful place, had to feel fresh air and sunshine on his face. He didn't remember using the elevator, but he must have, and then he was out in the parking lot, where he found their car and leaned against it and let the torrent break.

If any passersby noticed him, they didn't stop or speak. No doubt in this place where many people were deathly ill or dying, they were used to someone crying.

His parents found him there, he didn't know how much later.

"Marc. We couldn't find you," Dad said as they approached.

Had they even noticed that he was missing? he wondered. He must have been gone from Mallory's room for hours, and they'd only now come looking for him.

He stared at their drawn faces. "Is she dead?" he was compelled to ask, not really wanting to know the answer.

Shock registered on his mother's face. "Of course not! We're all praying with all our hearts, Marc! God won't let her die!"

"She thinks He will," Marc said. "He lets people die all the time, doesn't He? Why not Mallory?" Or me, he thought, or you, or anybody.

"Don't talk that way," Mrs. Solie said, sounding cross. "And for heaven's sake don't say anything like that in front of *her*."

"She said it to me," Marc told them as Dad pulled out his car keys. "She said she wouldn't be here the next time Dad and I came down."

It was as if he'd struck his mother. When the car door was opened, she sank into the passenger seat as if her legs had given out beneath her. She had remarked earlier that she was all cried out, but from the depths of her soul the grief reemerged, and she collapsed forward over her knees.

Hank Solie didn't immediately start the engine. He enfolded his wife in his arms, not really noticing as Marc climbed into the backseat.

They don't even remember that I'm here, Marc

thought. They're so wrapped up in their own agony that they don't even know I share it.

He never prayed for Mallory again.

He and Dad stayed in San Francisco at a motel over the weekend, and Marc went back to the hospital two more times. He listened to his parents expressing their love and concern for his little sister, heard their encouraging, hopeful words, and knew they were meaningless. He didn't seek or get another chance to talk to Mallory by himself. It was as if he were invisible, a sort of semighost watching from the sidelines, no longer part of the family at all.

And, Marc reflected bleakly as he sat now on that isolated Northern California hillside in the meager shade, he never did feel part of it again.

How had he wound up here, scared out of his wits, exhausted, hungry and thirsty, a fugitive from the police? If the cops weren't looking for him now, they soon would be.

Would the guards at the camp notify them at once, when they found Stoner's body? They'd have to notify somebody about Klammer, wouldn't they? Klammer was dead too, and it was Stoner's fault. They couldn't just bury him out on the hillside and pretend he'd never existed. His folks would have to be notified, and though they had sent him to Camp Heritage in the first place, which was a pretty good indication they didn't think much of him, surely they'd be interested in the fact that he had died, and would want to know what happened.

The Heritage staff was supposed to discipline and straighten out delinquent boys, not leave them to die of sunstroke or whatever Klammer had died of.

Marc hadn't liked Klammer—the guy was a bully and a jerk—but he hadn't deserved to die.

Marc had arrived in camp under the same presumption as everyone else: that he was a problem, incorrigible, out of control. He couldn't say they'd treated him any better or worse than any other boy at Heritage, even though most of the others were thugs and hoodlums.

How had he himself come to be so regarded? He never meant to be a source of fear and hatred and animosity. He would never have believed his mother would let anyone incarcerate him in such a place. All he'd wanted was to be a human being again, a person with needs and feelings.

"Well," he told the mutt licking his hand with a raspy tongue, "I've sure got needs and feelings now. And we've rested long enough. We better find that interstate, and head toward Dad."

He didn't say "toward home." He didn't really have a home anymore. Not unless Dad was willing and able to give him one.

He didn't know for sure how far he had to go. He was still in California, he knew that much, and when he got into Oregon he thought he'd be about three hundred miles from the Washington border, and then it would probably be another two hundred miles to Seattle. So, there was a total of between five and six hundred miles to go.

Doing it on foot was going to be close to impossible. He had no food, no water, no money.

He wondered how long it took to starve to death. He knew you could go longer without food than without water, but the only water he'd şeen so far—or knew about—was in Lake Shasta, a mile below his present altitude, and virtually inaccessible. He'd seen the lake on the way into Heritage, and under other circumstances he'd have thought it strikingly beautiful. But when you were on your way to exile—to prison, really—it was hard to be appreciative of even spectacular scenery.

I didn't deserve to be sent to Heritage. I never did anything that bad. Not like most of the other guys.

His mind was suddenly flooded with hatred for Floyd, who had put him there, knowing he wasn't a rapist or a mugger or a big-time thief. He had just been a scared and lonely kid who wanted nothing more than for someone to notice that he was alive, to restore to him the love and comfort of being part of a family.

The thought of Floyd gave him that little extra bit of strength he needed as he set out once more to climb the mountainside, in search of the interstate.

3

It was impossible to keep his mind blank while he climbed.

How could a near-perfect life have disintegrated so totally? He'd had plenty of time to think since Floyd had brought him up here to Heritage, but he'd never been able to figure it out.

It never would have happened if Mallory hadn't gotten sick. She was wrong about dying before he and Dad went down to San Francisco the next time. She lasted another three weeks, while Mom and Dad and the church congregations all counted on healing that never came.

Marc watched them all, disassociated from everything. He did his schoolwork, more or less, though his teachers expressed concern that his grades were slipping. Still, anybody could understand how he might be distracted by the fact that his sister and his mother were hundreds of miles away in a hospital from which his sister would never return.

Marc was the only one realistic enough to acknowledge that. Mallory knew. If she prayed at all, and he didn't know if she did, it was not for healing but for a quick release from what had become a painful life.

He didn't take her any more presents. There was no

point in having more stuff to carry back from San Francisco when the time came. They did bring back the white and black striped plush tiger, but when his mother placed it in Mallory's room, Marc made no move to reclaim it.

In spite of what had preceded it, the end took Patty Solie by surprise. She was in shrieking denial when the nurse pulled the sheet up over the small, pale face.

"No! No, God wouldn't let her die! We prayed and PRAYED FOR HER!"

Marc thought his dad had been expecting it. He struggled to control his own weariness and grief as he held his wife, who beat upon his chest as if he were the cause of their child's demise. It was not until a nurse came and administered an injection that Patty eventually subsided.

If anyone noticed that Marc was in the room when his sister died, there was no recognition of him. He stood to one side, ignored, while his parents were allowed to say their final good-byes to Mallory. He followed them— forgotten and unbidden—out of the hospital and back to the motel room. He stood by while his father made phone calls and arrangements after his mother had passed out on the ugly blue and green spread. He put their belongings back into the suitcases they'd carried back and forth for weeks now, and nobody reminded him that he might have forgotten anything.

Dad drove back to Eureka like an automaton, while his wife slumped in a drug-induced stupor that did not stem the flow of tears.

Marc sat in the backseat, dry-eyed, staring out at the deep green passing forests; interspersed by glimpses of the Eel River where it crossed and recrossed Highway 101.

He expected, naively, that sooner or later they'd pull themselves together and get back to normal.

It never happened.

The white tiger was placed on the pillow on Mallory's bed, because she had been holding it when she passed away, and it was sacred.

In fact, everything Mallory had ever touched was sacred to Patty.

No attempt was made to empty out her closets and drawers and pass along her clothes or her toys to needy children. The door to her room was kept closed, but Marc was only too aware that it sat as Mallory had left it.

School was out for the summer, and when Marc left the house no one asked where he was going, or with whom, or when he would return.

Supper time, when they had all used to gather and talk about their days and their interests, deteriorated into individuals scrounging whatever they could find in the refrigerator and heating up leftovers—when Patty had bothered to cook—in the microwave.

Dust settled on everything, except in Mallory's room.

Once Marc went to a movie with some of his buddies, and it was so good they all decided to stay and watch it a second time. It was nearly eight o'clock when he got home, and nobody so much as noticed. There was no indication that a meal had ever been prepared or served.

He heard his parents talking in their bedroom, but neither of them emerged while Marc made a peanut butter and jelly sandwich and scraped the last of the chocolate chip out of the ice cream carton. He finally went to bed without seeing them.

On Saturday, when Hank was always home from work, he and Marc had cold cereal and then he said purposefully, "What do you say we grab the vacuum cleaner and a dust cloth and repair a few of the ravages around here, buddy?"

Marc stared at his father. "Isn't Mom ever going to do any housework again, Dad?"

After a moment of silence, Hank said, "I don't know, son. I don't know."

"You're handling it by going back to work. Why can't Mom?"

Hank sighed. "Everybody's different, Marc. She's doing the best she can."

As they put the house in order, Patty never came out of the bedroom. At lunchtime Marc and his dad decided they needed to make a run to the supermarket.

Patty had always been conscious of the nutritional value of foods. Since she was making no attempt to cook, Marc and his father chose a lot more convenience and junk food than they could normally have gotten away with.

She refused to return to church, though many members brought food after the funeral, and called and sent cards. She didn't want to talk to anybody, and Marc felt awkward and inadequate when he had to deal with any of them. What was he supposed to say?

One evening she did come to the table when they announced that they were having tomato soup and toasted cheese sandwiches. She was picking at her food when Hank began tentatively, "I heard about Carl Forsythe's little girl today. Her name's Lensey. I think she's about seven, a little older than Mallory was, but she's small for her age. She's in the hospital now—she had an appendectomy. It occurred to me that she might be able to wear some of Mallory's stuff."

Patty put down her spoon and stared across the table in disbelief.

"Are you out of your mind?" she demanded.

Hank also forgot to eat, and Marc felt the familiar numbness begin to creep over him.

"She's a nice little kid, and she's just been through a rough time. I thought it might cheer her up—"

"A 'rough time'? With an appendectomy?"

"Honey, because we lost our own child doesn't mean we can't have any consideration for someone else's child. . . ."

An angry flush climbed into Patty's face. "How dare you! How dare you ask me to give up all I have left of my daughter for some child I don't even know! How dare you!"

Marc felt his throat tighten, his hands clench in his lap. His chest was constricted, making it hard to breathe.

Both of them were completely unaware of him as he sat between them, their attention only on each other.

"Mallory's gone," Hank said. "We can't bring her back by hanging on to all her stuff—"

Patty's shriek made Marc want to cover his ears. "No! Don't you touch anything of Mallory's! Never!"

Marc watched his dad strive for control, barely achieving it. "Patty, be reasonable. I'm not saying we have to give her things to this little girl today, or even next week, but sooner or later we're going to have to clear out her room. It can't stay a shrine forever—that's not healthy for any of us."

"It's healthy for me," Patty informed him, in no way pacified. "She was the only daughter I'll ever have, and I have a right to keep all her things to remember her by."

"Honey, we don't need things to remember Mallory. She was my daughter too, and I loved her so much I thought I'd die too when it happened. But we don't need clothes and toys to keep her in our hearts."

Patty shoved back her chair and stood up, making everybody's soup slop over onto the table. Her voice dropped so low that if they'd been a few feet farther away they wouldn't have heard it. "Don't you ever make such a demand on me again, ever. Do you understand me, Hank? Not ever. I will not give up one precious thing."

She turned and stalked away, her body rigid, and Marc listened to his own breathing and realized his father's had been suspended.

My sister died, and now my mother's gone crazy, Marc thought. He moistened his lips and waited for his dad to speak. To his horror, he saw that Dad, who'd always been the strong one, the one able to fix anything, had tears in his eyes.

Marc couldn't ask what they were going to do,

because Hank didn't seem to have any idea at all.

The next day—for what reason he couldn't have explained—Marc tried the door to his sister's room and found it locked. Maybe his dad tried it too, because later Marc heard his parents discussing it.

They were in their room, and he stopped to listen, because their voices reflected the same strain he was feeling and he wanted to know what they were going to do about this situation that was tearing their family apart long after they should have started healing.

Dad's voice was clear and firm as his words reached his son. "Why did you lock the door?"

"How do you know it's locked unless you tried to go in there?"

"I did intend to look inside. She was my daughter too, Patty. I wanted to look at her belongings."

"You want to give them away. I won't do it, Hank. I won't unlock the door."

"Patricia." There was a new quality to his voice. "I think it's time we talked to Pastor Collins about this . . . obsession you have about Mallory's belongings."

"It's none of his business," Mom said at once, and there was no yielding in her tone.

"We're all grieving, but this goes beyond natural sorrow—can't you see that? We need to talk to someone who can be objective—"

"Someone who'll convince me I'm abnormal because I don't want to dispose of my daughter's clothes and toys? You expect too much of me."

"I want us to be a family again, Patty. We still have a

son, we're still husband and wife, and we're all desperately unhappy. This has been going on long enough. We need to see a counselor—if not Pastor Collins, then someone else."

"Someone who'll talk me around to your way of thinking, you mean. I suppose you've already discussed this with Pastor and that he agrees with you."

"I haven't discussed it with anyone, and it seems we can't discuss it between us. Patty, please, for the sake of our marriage and our family, consider talking to someone. You can pick out the counselor if you don't want to go to Ron Collins."

"I don't need a counselor to tell me how to grieve for my daughter, or to tell me it's unhealthy to keep Mallory's belongings. Leave me alone, Hank. I just want you to leave me alone."

"How can I leave you alone when you're so irrational? You've stopped doing all the normal things a woman does in a home. You don't cook. You don't worry about the laundry. You refuse to go to church—"

"I went to church, and I prayed, and I asked everybody else to pray with me. And she died anyway, Hank! She died anyway!"

"So are you saying that because God didn't answer those specific prayers the way we wanted Him to that you don't believe in Him anymore?"

"I'm saying you have no right to try to force me to go to church when I don't want to."

"You're shutting us out, Patty—Marc and me. Don't you care anything about what *we're* going through?"

Their words went on and on, and Marc stood paralyzed, not wanting to hear them, unable to move from the spot. Finally the words dissolved into weeping that shredded his spirit as if someone had taken a knife and plunged it into him over and over until he was near collapse himself.

He finally went on to bed and lay for a long time in the dark, unable to sleep, or pray, or cry. He could only hurt in every bone and muscle and tissue, a hurt every bit as bad as he'd felt when he'd first been convinced that his sister was dying.

It was the following day, when he'd been walking through the back alley, wondering how he was going to survive, or even if he was going to survive, that the impotent rage swept over him, out of control.

He wanted to kill something; to physically tear out the pain and make it go away, and he reached for the first thing he saw. He picked up a rock and threw it with all his strength, not caring where it hit or what it broke. And then another rock, and another, and even the sound of smashing glass didn't stop him until he'd exhausted himself and sank into a sobbing heap in the middle of the alley.

"Hey! What the devil do you think you're doing? You broke two of my windows and there's glass all over inside my house!"

The neighbor—Marc didn't remember his name—ran right up to him and stood staring down at him. "What's the matter with you? Aren't you the Solie kid? I'm going to tell your dad I expect him to pay for the damage. Consider yourself lucky nobody got hurt by flying glass."

Marc scarcely heard him, engrossed as he was in his own distress, doubled over in a ball. "Hey," the man said again, "what's wrong with you? Are you hurt? Sick?"

Yes, sick, Marc thought, and there was no shot or pill that was going to make anything better.

The anger had faded from the man's voice. "I'm going to get your folks," he said, and Marc heard his feet crunching in the gravel as he moved away.

His mother came. She'd pulled on an old sweater over her slacks and blouse, for summers were cool in Eureka, situated as it was on the seacoast. "I'm sorry," she was saying to the neighbor. "I'll see that his father takes care of it."

Some of the man's annoyance had returned. "He's old enough to know you can't go around breaking people's windows, no matter how bad he feels," he said. "You need help getting him home?"

By this time Marc had stopped crying. He wiped his nose on his bare arm and summoned up enough reason to get to his feet. "I'm sorry," he muttered, not looking at either of them. "I couldn't stand it anymore."

"My daughter just died," Patty told the neighbor. "He's upset. We're sorry, we'll pay for the damages."

"Oh, well . . . I'm sorry about that, but you can't go around lashing out and breaking windows, boy. You have to find a better way to handle it." He hesitated, then said, "Maybe you ought to consider taking him to someone. You know, a counselor or something."

"I'll talk to my husband," Mom said. She didn't speak to Marc as they walked home together. Marc never knew if she mentioned the incident to his dad or not, but neither of them ever said another word to him about a counselor.

He almost wished they had.

4

The afternoon sun burned through the shirt on his back
and he wished he had a bandanna to tie around his
forehead to keep the sweat out of his eyes. There was no
sound except his own labored breathing as he climbed,
occasionally skidding backward on the rocks that moved
under his feet.

Rat trotted beside him, tongue hanging out.

And then, suddenly, there was something. Marc
stopped, clutching a ragged bush.

Above his head, not very far away, he heard the sound
of an engine.

"We did it!" he told the dog. "We got to the
interstate!"

Rat whimpered, and Marc dropped his free hand onto
the dog's head. "Now we have to take a chance—either
walk along the road and hope somebody picks us up, or
hide every time we hear a car coming in case they've got
an APB out on us already."

He was torn between the belief that the staff at Camp
Heritage would immediately call in the authorities and
the hope that they'd need time to scramble around and
come up with a good reason why one of the boys, as well
as a camp counselor—as they called them, though the
boys referred to them as guards—was dead. Once that

news was out, the cops would be swarming over the place, wouldn't they? Marc didn't think they really wanted police officers in their midst, poking into all the corners, asking questions.

The sight of Klammer's limp body flashed through his mind, along with his immediate conviction, once he'd determined the boy was lifeless, that he was next on the list of those who'd never walk away from Camp Heritage.

Well, he'd run away, and he'd taken Rat with him, against all odds. And now he could hear the cars on the highway above him. He didn't know what lies the staff would tell—about Klammer, about himself, about the fallen guard Stoner whose blood still stained Marc's hands—but he knew it was unlikely that anybody'd accept *his* version of what had taken place.

He'd wiped his hands on the coarse grass, but it was too stiff, too dry. He needed water to wash in, and there hadn't been any so far.

He began to climb again, the dog beside him. "I wish I had a leash for you," he told Rat. "I don't know if you've got any sense about cars or not. If you get out on the road you'll get hit, and that'll kill you."

He had nothing from which to fashion a leash, and Rat wore no collar; nobody bothered putting collars on puppies they abandoned to die. The other three had all been dead when they were found beside the road, weeks ago. It was a miracle he'd managed to keep this one alive, with resources for feeding him so limited. Plus, if Rat hadn't been so timid, hiding under Marc's cot in the barracks when the boy had to leave him, he'd have fallen afoul of Stoner earlier.

Stoner made no secret of his contempt for dogs. Marc couldn't even be sure it hadn't been Stoner who had tossed the puppies out of a moving vehicle originally. It could have been someone on the staff, because except for an occasional delivery van, nobody else used the road that led in to the camp. Stoner seemed a likely candidate, though Marc couldn't imagine how he'd have been in possession of a litter of pups in the first place.

"Hear it? Hear the traffic?" His excitement was rising, because they were close to their immediate goal, but there was fear, too. Fear of being caught, fear of being taken back to Camp Heritage.

But no, if they thought he'd killed Stoner they wouldn't take him back to camp—they'd take him to jail, wouldn't they? Where? In Redding, or some other town north of where they were now.

I-5 didn't carry as much traffic here as it did farther south, but from the sound of it, there were plenty of cars and trucks. He knew the trucks that his dad dispatched ran all the way from Seattle to Los Angeles, and he knew what they looked like: a distinctive bright blue on white, with the K & M Trucking logo on the doors. If he spotted one of them, and he was really lucky, the driver would know his dad, know who he was, anyway. Would such a driver give him a ride all the way to his destination? Without questioning what he was doing out here in the wild?

If he said he'd been in a vehicle that had run off the

road, they'd have to call the cops and report an accident. Anybody would know he was too young to have been driving alone, so they'd look for others who'd been hurt.

No, he'd have to think of something more credible than that.

Thirst tormented him, and breakfast was so far behind him his belly button was scratching his spine. When the vision of a juicy hamburger suddenly rose in his mind, he decided not to think about the impossible. But it was impossible not to dwell on his thirst.

He looked up, and there was an eighteen-wheeler roaring past, tall enough so that he could see the top of an orange trailer. *Please God, let there be a K & M truck!* Then he remembered that prayers were a waste of time. He kept climbing, and a moment later went over the guardrail on I-5, lifting Rat with him.

He didn't dare put him down—there was more traffic than he'd expected. A lot of it was tourists with trailers and motor homes and pickups with campers. The rest of it was trucks, but he didn't spot any from K & M, and he didn't know how he'd stop one of those if he saw it.

None of the drivers paid any attention to him. Marc waited for a break, then crossed the road to walk against traffic, heading north.

He'd been down I-5 several times with his dad, but he didn't remember it in any detail. He recalled a place called Castle Crags with spectacular rock formations far overhead, and he thought the next town of any size he'd come to would be Yreka, which wasn't very big either. They'd stopped at rest areas several times through this section, but he couldn't remember where any of them were.

There'd be water at a rest stop.

Rat wasn't a very big dog, but after a while, as cars and trucks and RVs whizzed past them at enviable speed, he got kind of heavy. And he emanated an unwelcome amount of heat.

Unexpectedly, they crossed a culvert, and there was a trickle of water in it.

Marc dropped to his knees and urged Rat toward the water, where he eagerly lapped at it. Only when his buddy had satisfied himself did Marc cup his hands to scoop up some for himself.

Never had a drink been more refreshing. He splashed some over his face, and then over his arms, and then he drank some more.

Before he stood up again, he soaked his T-shirt as well. The moisture quickly dried and cooled him down, at least for a few minutes.

A hundred yards farther along, he came upon a bungee cord lying on the shoulder.

Marc picked it up and fastened a sort of choke collar on Rat, so he could let the dog walk without danger of his moving in front of a lethal vehicle.

There: They were in better shape than they had been. They went on, and because there was little else to occupy his mind, Marc drifted back into memories.

Mom had gradually emerged from her room and begun to take over her old chores. She went to the grocery market and brought back things like fruits and vegetables that Marc and Hank had not been buying. She got out the vacuum cleaner, and scrubbed the tubs and sinks in the bathrooms. She sat down at the table and ate with them, regular meals with meat and salads and casseroles.

She didn't talk much, only when one of them asked her a question, and then she replied in monosyllables.

Marc wasn't sure when he realized that his father had moved out of the bedroom his parents had shared for as long as he could remember, and was sleeping on a couch in the study. Did this mean that except for the fact that his parents still lived under the same roof, the marriage was at an end? Was there now no chance at all they'd ever be a normal family again?

Dad hadn't given up on the idea of consulting a counselor, though. Several times, late at night when they thought he was asleep, Marc heard them. His father was urgent, pleading. His mother was adamant: There was nothing wrong with her. There was no reason to consult anybody.

She had always played the piano when she was stressed, though she'd stopped while Mallory was in the hospital. Now she resumed, especially when she thought no one was listening. Even though he didn't recognize most of the music, much of it was sad enough to make him cry.

Mostly, though, he put the tears behind him. And the rage he'd felt that day in the alley increased, and he felt the need to smash something, to destroy the perfection of anything that did not ease his pain.

His friend Toby poked him playfully in the belly out on the school grounds, and Marc hit him back, hard, before he thought.

Toby sprawled on the blacktop and looked up at him in astonishment. "Hey, man, what's wrong with you? I was just kidding."

"Sorry," Marc mumbled, "you took me by surprise." He was chagrined to realize that for a moment he'd felt like killing the other boy. He reached down a hand to pull Toby up, and they were friends again. But Marc's inner fury built and built until it made his head hurt and he was gritting his teeth a lot.

When they played games, Marc got rougher and rougher, until the other boys complained.

"What's wrong with you, Solie?" the coach demanded. "You got a bee in your bonnet you need to get rid of?" He had just slammed into Owen Smith so hard he'd bloodied his nose and sent him to the washroom.

"Sorry," Marc muttered again. But he wasn't sorry. Except for himself. Oh, yes, he was sorry for himself.

Nobody cared if he didn't go straight home after school, and he took to hanging around with the guys in the parking lot behind Rotten Robbie's where the high school kids congregated. He knew they were the kind of kids his parents would once have disapproved of, but since his folks paid him no attention anymore, what difference did it make?

They talked about different things than the middle school kids did. Girls, and drugs, and grudges, and small-time crimes they had committed, or thought about committing. Marc didn't know if they were making stuff up, or if they really did it, but it was kind of exciting to listen.

When one of them offered him a cigarette, Marc took it and accepted a light. About two inhalations into it he knew it was a mistake. He blew out the smoke and hoped he wouldn't throw up. He couldn't stop the coughing spell that followed, though.

The guys looked at him and grinned. "Does that to everybody," one of them said. "You'll get used to it."

No, Marc decided on his way home, he wouldn't get used to it. He remembered everything his family had told him about Grandpa Bill, who died of emphysema and congestive heart failure when Marc was about eight.

"Directly connected to a lifelong habit of smoking," his mother and grandmother had reported. "He got hooked, and he could never manage to stop. He was only seventy-two when he died, and he died by inches over several years, his breathing getting harder and harder until it just wore him out and he gave up."

Besides that, smoking was expensive, and Marc didn't have the money to pay for cigarettes even if he'd wanted them.

The minute he walked into the house, his mother sniffed. "Marc, I smell tobacco on you," she said accusingly.

"I was with some guys who were smoking," Marc said, not quite lying. "The smell sticks in your hair and your clothes."

"If I ever heard that you're smoking, it would kill

me," Mom said. "Your grandmother, too, after all she went through with Grandpa."

"Don't worry, I'm never gonna use anything I'd get addicted to," Marc told her, and he meant it.

It wasn't long after that that one of the older boys showed up with a bottle in a paper sack and passed it around. More cautious this time, expecting the worst, Marc sipped carefully when it was his turn.

He managed not to choke, but he didn't see why anybody'd drink the stuff. Not for the taste, that was for sure. His throat burned as if he'd poured acid down it, then turned just hot.

"Have a bigger snort," the owner of the bottle urged. "You didn't get enough to loosen you up, Solie."

He wanted loosening up, so he took another swallow. And after a while it did make him feel kind of funny, if that was what "loosening up" was. When another boy suggested they all go into Pop's Corner Cage—so called because of the grilles over the windows and the door when he was closed—and mill around to distract the old man while some of them filched a few goodies, Marc was stupid enough to go along.

In spite of the liquor he'd ingested, he knew it was stupid. But oddly enough it was kind of exciting to be with these older guys, and briefly his inner pain had receded. He'd never spent much time in Pop's—it was a small store, with lots of junk he'd been taught not to eat, and it was crowded, and the proprietor was crabby—but he went in and stuck a bag of chips under his shirt. He got out with it before Pop could detect the bulge, involved as he was in an altercation with a couple of the older guys over their change.

They all grinned approvingly when they gathered again outside. He shared the chips, and the other stuff they had stolen.

Later, though, on the way home, he felt shame. He knew stealing was wrong. "Don't do it to the other guy if you're not prepared to have him do it to you," Dad had told him, more than once.

It was the alcohol, Marc decided. While it had made him feel a little better for a while, kind of too muzzy to worry about how miserable his life had become, once the drink began to wear off he felt worse. Crummy and stupid and ashamed.

He made it a point not to get close enough to either parent when he got home for them to smell him. No matter how neglectful they had become, they wouldn't overlook the obvious odor of alcohol, and he couldn't claim that had settled over him while he was a bystander.

He thought he was fully cognizant of the situation between his parents, but he wasn't prepared to learn they were divorcing.

His dad told him. "It breaks my heart, son, but I can't go on like this. I've tried everything I know. Your mother refused counseling, so I went by myself and talked to Pastor Collins; he, too, thinks Mom's obsession in keeping Mallory's room just the way she left it is unhealthy. And she refuses to have anything more to do with me than asking me to pass the salt. I can't do it anymore."

Marc was frozen in disbelief. Things had been bad

before, but now they had gone on to worse. "But . . . where will we go? What will we do?" *What will happen to me?* he wanted to ask, but couldn't.

"Your mother will stay on here in the house, and you'll stay with her. I've got a room rented; I'll be moving out over the weekend. I don't want to stay in Eureka—it's too small a town and we'd run into each other all the time—so I'm going to look for work somewhere else. They need experienced dispatchers for trucking firms practically everywhere, and I'm thinking around Seattle, where my mother is."

Marc's alarm bells were screaming in every direction. "But what about me? I won't even see you if you move to Seattle!"

"I'll make contact as often as I can. We can always stay in touch with e-mail and the phone. Maybe, once I get settled, if it works out, Mom will consider giving me custody of you and you can come live with me. I don't want to fight her in court on it now, son—she's so fragile, I don't think she could handle it."

Neither can I! Marc wanted to yell, but he couldn't. His throat had closed and he could hardly breathe.

"I don't want to take you out of school here until I'm sure we can work it out up there. You're not really old enough to be alone when I'm tied up at work," Dad said.

But I'm as good as alone now! Nobody pays any attention to me! I've been invisible since Mallory got sick, and if you move away and leave me here I'll die too! The words formed in his mind but stuck there, refusing to be spoken aloud.

So the words were not said, and Dad moved out, and

within a week he called to report that he'd talked to Grandma Belle and he was going to stay with her while he scouted around for a job. "Don't worry, you'll be fine with Mom," he said.

And then there were only the two of them in the house, Marc and his mother, and of course the ghost of Mallory, locked in that room with the white plush tiger and her books and her pretty little-girl clothes.

Mom fixed his meals. She washed his clothes. She told him to take shorter showers because he was using up all the hot water. She did not ask where he was going, or when he was coming home, or who he was spending time with. She did not talk about the games he played or the movies he went to or the book he was currently reading.

She played the sad music on the piano and did not answer the phone, so Marc had to tell people she wasn't available, and pretty soon the old friends from church stopped calling, and the neighbors stopped dropping by to visit or commiserate.

And every day Marc fell deeper into depression and despondency, and became more and more helpless to do anything to save himself.

5

Floyd Dunning came to the house to talk to Marc's mother about insurance.

Marc disliked him on sight.

Floyd wasn't anything like Dad, who was tall and of athletic build and liked to laugh a lot—at least until Mallory got sick.

Floyd wore suits and was getting a bit thick through the middle, though he wasn't really fat yet. His fair hair was thinning on top, always carefully combed straight back as if he thought that would keep anyone from noticing.

He drove a big dark blue Cadillac, two years old but quite elegant. A man in the insurance business needs to keep up appearances with a good car, Marc heard him tell Patty Solie.

His mother had put on makeup for the first time in a long while, in preparation for his visit. She looked strange to Marc's eyes, after his having seen her for so long without even lipstick. He couldn't have said why, but she made him nervous in this new/old persona.

"What's the occasion?" he asked before Floyd showed up.

"No occasion. There's a man coming to discuss insurance, that's all. Comb your hair and wash up, Marc. You look like a bum."

"Well, at least you noticed," he said, on the way to the bathroom. She made no response to that, busying herself with clearing off the dining room table so they could work there when the insurance agent came.

Marc glanced in later, after he'd heard the doorbell ring. He didn't know why he'd bothered to wash and comb his hair; when he stood in the doorway his mother paid no attention to him and didn't introduce him.

Floyd was there for nearly two hours, explaining and demonstrating what sounded like very dull stuff. When he stood at last and started putting papers into his briefcase, he said, "I'll work this up and come back Friday night, if that's all right?"

"Yes, of course," Patty said. "I really appreciate your coming to the house. It was much easier than for me to go to an office somewhere. I don't really get out much since my daughter passed away."

Floyd smiled, and though Marc was once more within hearing range, he wasn't introduced then, either. "No problem, Mrs. Solie. I'll look into that other matter and let you know about that, too."

She walked him to the door, and closed it behind him. Marc had by that time turned on the TV and was watching the end of a ball game; he thought no more about it.

And then twice the next week he came home from school and found the blue Caddie out front. What was up? How much insurance did they need?

The second time Marc saw that they were sitting in the living room, side by side on the couch, drinking coffee. As if it were a social visit. The briefcase was on the coffee table, unopened. Marc heard Floyd laugh softly, as if his mother had said something amusing.

Amusing? His mother? Marc's uncertainty and uneasiness increased.

Somebody broke into Pop's Corner Cage that weekend, and a pair of detectives were at school, asking questions. Nobody admitted to knowing anything about it, though Marc had his suspicions. Some of the bunch who had swiped stuff before had talked about maybe hitting the place, though they hadn't asked him to participate this time.

When the police officer talked to his class Marc made no move to respond to the plea for information. Neighbors had seen boys, and it was reasonable to assume they attended either the middle or high school. The officer wrote his phone number on the board, where it stayed for a week, and assured the students they could speak with him in confidence if they chose.

Nothing happened to indicate that anyone squealed. According to the news, the police were continuing their investigation, but no arrests had been made.

Arrests. If he'd been caught with the potato chips, he'd have been arrested. His dad would have been really upset. Marc decided to slack off on hanging around with the group he'd shoplifted with, whom he was sure had been involved in this latest incident.

He drifted back toward Toby and the others he'd hung out with before, but they were all happily engaged in sports and bogging down with homework. It was uncomfortable listening to them complain about parents who were concerned about them, setting and enforcing limits on their comings and goings. After the high school kids, those his own age seemed childish and immature.

Marc kept in touch with his dad, mostly by e-mail. Dad found another job as a dispatcher with K & M Trucking, and for the time being was going to stay at Grandma's house. He'd continue to send support checks to Marc and his mother. He said nothing about having Marc join him, and Marc was afraid to ask.

The school year limped along, with Marc's grades falling, mostly because he found the work boring and didn't try very hard. He stopped doing any of the extra-credit work that had always kept him at the top of his class, burying himself instead in reading or watching TV shows that took no effort. He slept more than usual. He was overtired, though he did little to get that way.

One day in the spring he arrived home, walked past the blue Cadillac, and found Floyd and his mother in the kitchen, on opposite sides of the table. Floyd had his back to Marc as he came in the door, and he said earnestly, "You really ought to consider selling the house, Patricia. It would be the sensible thing to do. It's much too big for the two of you, and too expensive to keep up."

He'd gone from "Mrs. Solie" to "Patricia." Marc scowled, heading for the refrigerator. He saw his mother's face as he passed her chair—pale, immediately in denial.

"I can't sell it, Floyd. All of Mallory's belongings are here. It's the only home she ever had."

"It's been a year," Floyd said gently. "You can't really afford to keep the place, Patricia. Look, you think about it, seriously, and when I come back on Saturday we'll talk about it."

He was coming back on Saturday? And he wanted her to sell the house, where Mallory's bedroom was still locked against any intruder?

Marc's appetite had instantly diminished, but he made a sandwich anyway, and peeled an orange, and went out in the backyard to eat. As the door closed behind him, he heard his mother say, "Don't make me, Floyd. Please, don't make me."

Make her? How could an insurance salesman make her do anything, when Dad hadn't been able to talk her around?

Later, when he sent an e-mail to his dad, he summoned the nerve to mention Floyd.

"There's this guy who's coming around," Marc wrote. "He was selling insurance, and his name's Floyd Dunning, and today when he came he didn't have his briefcase or anything that looked like business. He calls Mom Patricia, now, and she calls him Floyd. I don't think it's about insurance anymore. I think it's personal."

And Dad wrote back: "She's not married to me any longer, son. She's free to see anybody she likes."

"Is the divorce final, then?" Marc asked. It was a little easier to ask in writing what he couldn't put into words when they spoke on the phone or in person. The thought made him slightly sick to his stomach. He knew that lots of kids' parents got divorced, but he'd never dreamed it would happen in his own family.

"Well, it will be soon. I'm sorry, son. I know it hurts, but we couldn't go on the way we were."

Marc's throat ached. He couldn't say he understood. He didn't understand anything. Not why Mallory had gotten leukemia, why the prayers hadn't worked, why his parents had both taken it so hard and yet had no common ground in their grief. Not why other parents were able to get past the sorrow and his mother hadn't been able to, hadn't been able to see that there was no bringing Mallory back or keeping her "alive" by hanging on to everything the child had ever touched.

Gathering all the courage he could muster, Marc typed, "I don't belong here now, Dad. I don't belong anywhere. Nobody wants me now."

The answer came back quickly. "I want you, son. I can't have you with me right now, but that situation won't last forever. I pray for you every day, every morning and every night before I go to sleep."

He couldn't write, *What difference does that make? We all prayed for Mallory, too. If God didn't care about her, why should He care about me?*

When he didn't respond in a moment or two, Dad came back with his own gentle reminder. "God answered our prayers about your sister, Marc, just not in the way we wanted. I asked your mother, would you want her to go on living, suffering the way she is? Mallory was ready to go, to end the pain and the fear. I think there at the end she was asking God to take her, to give her peace. But your mom couldn't handle that. It was hard for me to handle too, but if I'd had a choice, I wouldn't have extended her life when it was clear she wasn't going to get well. God takes everybody sooner or later, son. It's the end part of life, for everybody on the planet."

The words came again, painful, bringing tears to Marc's eyes. "But Mallory was only a little girl. Why was she punished that way?"

"Little girls go to heaven, the same as the rest of us. And I don't guess God considers that a punishment, to take us on to a better life than we've had on this earth. Don't lose faith, son, just because your mother has. She can't help it, but you still can."

Marc couldn't admit how far gone he was in that regard. Usually he felt a mixture of gratification and sadness at the physical separation between them when he and his dad "talked" via computer. Today the satisfaction was missing, because he was still here, and Floyd kept coming to the house, ignoring Marc but sweet-talking his mother. He was afraid to know what Floyd's intentions were.

It got so that when Marc came home and saw the blue Caddie parked in front, he went around to the kitchen and came in the back door to get a snack before he escaped to his room, hoping not to encounter them at all. Sometimes they were sitting at the kitchen table, though, drinking endless cups of coffee, and he couldn't avoid them. Sometimes they stopped talking when he was near. Other times, he heard Floyd sympathizing with his mother or otherwise backing her stand on one point or another.

"Hank didn't care," Marc heard her say once. "Mallory was gone and he could just forget it. But I can't, Floyd!"

Dad didn't care? How could Mom be so much more anguished that she was oblivious to everybody else's pain? Neither he nor Dad had had hysterics or screamed their grief to the world, but surely she couldn't have suffered that much more than they had.

Floyd had leaned across the table, paying no attention to Marc as he built his baloney and mustard sandwich at the counter, and reached for Patricia's hand. "I can only imagine how terrible it must have been for you. I have two daughters of my own—Barbara and Annette—and I know I would be devastated if anything happened to either of them. But some people are callous about others' pain."

How unfair could you get? To minimize Dad's grief, just because he wanted to get on with his life since he couldn't do a thing about losing his beloved child. *And neither Mom nor Floyd even considers that I had a loss too.* Marc seethed, and, paying no attention to what he was doing, slathered mustard all over his hand.

He would have loved to turn around and strike them both with whatever he could grab—the frying pan still sitting on the stove with a spatula in it, the pot of herbs growing on the windowsill, his bare fists.

He couldn't hit them, so he grabbed his sandwich and let himself out the back door, slamming it behind him.

He heard his mother's protest—"Marc, how many times have I told you . . ."—but he didn't stop or apologize. They were so unfair! And Floyd wasn't trying to get Mom over this dreadful state she was in, he was encouraging it!

He'd been hungry before he made the sandwich, but now he looked at it with loathing. If he ate it, he'd puke it back up. His stomach was roiling, demanding release of his anger and frustration.

The garbage can on the back porch, emptied that morning, was in his way. Instead of going around it, Marc kicked it down the steps, where the lid rolled off and away, clattering.

Now his toes hurt, but he welcomed the misery. If he could, he'd kick down the whole darned house, with them inside it.

He went through the yard to the alley, threw his sandwich over the fence to the Griswolds' pit bull, and ran. Maybe, he thought, if he ran far enough and fast enough, he could outrun everything that weighed him down.

He faltered to a stop eventually, collapsing on the bleachers at the school athletic field. His lungs were on fire, but he welcomed that, too. If the physical pain was bad enough, maybe it would drown out the emotional anguish.

Some older guys crossed the field, spotting him. "Hey, Solie!" one of them called. "Want to go out to the beach with us? We're gonna cut some wheelies!"

Marc sucked in air, willing a calm he didn't feel. "Sure, why not? What're you driving?"

"Jake's got his brother's Jeep. You got any money for gas, by any chance?"

Money. A distant part of his mind was aware that the older guys never paid any attention to him unless they wanted something. But he'd just gotten his allowance, and he had it in his pocket. "Sure," he said, "I can chip in a few bucks."

So they piled in the Jeep, the four of them and Marc, and he handed over a five-dollar bill for gas, and they went out onto the spit.

The beaches were clean white sand, broad and firm at low tide, and after a while Marc loosened up and laughed with the others, yelling as they dug circles in the sand, almost rolling the vehicle. Then they did roll it, and this time the pain was excruciating, as Marc landed with his arm underneath him and he heard a bone crack.

Somebody swore, and Marc saw blood on the forehead of the boy who'd been driving—he couldn't even remember what his name was—but everybody was still alive. After a few minutes of more general swearing and sorting themselves out, some of them were laughing as they set about turning the Jeep back on its wheels.

"Come on, Solie, lift," one of them urged, and he tried, but fell back.

"I think my arm's broke," Marc said.

There was more swearing, but he didn't think anybody really cared about it except himself.

They got the Jeep upright, and decided they'd had enough fun for one session; besides, it was getting dark, and it got cold on the beach at night in Eureka. "I'd better get this thing home before my brother gets back from Crescent City," the driver said, "and hope he doesn't notice the new dings in it."

"You mean he doesn't even know you have it?" someone asked.

"You think he's crazy enough to let me drive his precious Iron Horse? I gotta get it back where he left it before he gets home. You want us to take you home, Solie? You really think your arm is broken?"

It was beginning to ache intensely. "Yeah," Marc said, "I think it's broke."

So they took him home, and he got about the reception he expected, and of course Floyd was there to witness his disgrace.

6

It was fully dark by the time he got home, and sure enough, his luck was typical: The blue Caddie was still parked in the driveway. After listening to the guys with the "borrowed" Jeep, Marc didn't have any trouble coming up with a few cusswords of his own.

There was no sneaking past his mother this time: He had to have something done with his arm.

There were the remains of a meal on the kitchen table. Spaghetti and meatballs, salad, steamed broccoli and carrots. Even lemon cake with cream cheese frosting. At least the food had improved since Floyd had begun staying for dinner.

They both stared at him accusingly. "Where have you been? Dinnertime was over two hours ago," his mother stated, rising to her feet. Floyd stood up too, looking out of sorts, as if he were Marc's father.

"I was on the beach with some guys, and they rolled the Jeep. I've got a broken arm, I think," Marc said.

If he had any hope that a fracture might win him sympathy, he was quickly disabused of the notion.

"Rolled the Jeep! Marc, you know you're not allowed to ride in anyone's car without permission! What were you thinking? You might have been killed!"

"It wasn't likely—the sand is soft. Can we—can we

go to the emergency room and get it fixed?"

"It wasn't soft enough to keep it from breaking your arm," Floyd observed. "I'll take you, Patricia. You'd better get a sweater—there's no telling how long it will take. I'll have to call my girls and tell them I'll be late." He fixed a malevolent eye on Marc, standing there hanging on to his left arm as if that might ease the pain. "I wouldn't have stayed *this* long except that your mother was worried that you hadn't come home when you were supposed to. We didn't know where to look for you, and I didn't want to leave her alone. This was pretty inconsiderate of you, son."

Marc wanted to point out that he wasn't Floyd's son, but this probably wasn't the best time to argue.

"I'll call ahead, ask Dr. Uvaldi to meet us at the hospital," Patricia said. "I can't believe you were so irresponsible, Marc. Your father would be so ashamed of you."

You don't have the faintest idea how my father feels about anything, Marc thought, but he didn't think it would be wise to contest that statement either.

So he got a ride to the hospital in the now-hated Cadillac, with its plush deep blue upholstery and carpet, and they X-rayed his arm after they'd all three sat waiting until the victims of a real car accident had been taken care of. As they watched them wheeled past on gurneys, liberally bloodied about their heads and torsos, Patricia turned pale.

"They're not much older than you are, Marc, and look at the results of careless driving! I've already lost one child, and I could easily have lost the only one I have left!"

"Mom, I just broke my arm. I could have done it falling down the stairs at home. Don't make such a big deal out of it," Marc said, wishing with all his heart that his dad were here instead of Floyd. Dad had broken an ankle playing basketball when he was a little older than Marc was now, and he'd smashed up his father's car, driving too fast, when he was seventeen, and had suffered a concussion. And he didn't panic in an emergency.

Floyd cleared his throat. "Don't be rude to your mother, young man."

Rude? Marc wanted to show him rude, but he didn't quite dare.

"Does that mean I'm not allowed to speak at all?" he managed.

"If you can't be civil, yes," Floyd said, and Marc wanted to know what in heck this man considered "civil."

Finally a nurse called them into a sort of cubicle formed by hanging curtains, which did nothing to muffle the sounds from both sides. To Marc's left someone was throwing up, and on his right someone was begging for a shot to stop the pain.

They waited again, an interminable period, and finally the doctor came. "Sorry for the delay. One of those kids from the car wreck was a patient of mine too," Dr. Uvaldi said. "What have we here, Marc?"

"Broken arm, I think," Marc told him. "I was in a Jeep that rolled, out on the spit."

After that he was coerced into a wheelchair for a ride to the X-ray department. "Hey, I walked in here! I can walk that far," he protested, but was overruled.

His arm was aching pretty bad, and he wondered when they'd give him something for the pain. Once the pictures were finished, Dr. Uvaldi returned and looked them over. "Yep, greenstick fracture," he said. "You're lucky, Marc. Could have been a lot worse. We can give you a nice removable cast, so you can take a shower if you're careful and don't fall down in the tub and make it worse." He sounded incredibly cheerful, but of course it wasn't his fracture.

"What about the pain?" Marc dared to ask.

"Pain is one of the results of stupidity," Floyd offered before the doctor could reply. "Some things you just learn to live with."

Dr. Uvaldi had known the family ever since Marc was a baby, and he knew that Marc's dad would never have said something like that to the boy. He spoke directly to Marc. "I'll write you out a prescription; you can fill it on your way home. It'll enable you to sleep tonight. You probably won't need it for long. Just avoid falling on it or bumping it again, okay?"

The cast was not plaster but plastic and nylon, and it came with a sling. Marc didn't know whether to be grateful that his mother had finally noticed she still had one kid, or annoyed that she was making such a fuss. When he was little and got hurt, he'd sort of enjoyed being fussed over, but he seemed to have outgrown that.

He hoped Floyd would simply leave them off at the

front door and go home, but he didn't. Marc needed to use the bathroom and decided on the one downstairs instead of going all the way upstairs, and when he came out their voices came to him clearly from the kitchen, where the supper table was finally being cleared away.

"You know, maybe he'd be happier with his own father," Floyd said.

"Oh, Hank doesn't want him! He's too busy with his own life," Patricia said.

Marc halted, disbelieving. That wasn't true, was it? Surely Dad had never told her that?

His mouth dry, feeling shaky all over, he climbed the stairs to his room. The pill he'd swallowed hadn't taken hold yet, but the ache he felt in his heart was worse than the pain in his arm, and a few tears leaked through before he was able to go to sleep.

Crying, of course, hadn't improved the situation then, and didn't improve it now as he moved alongside the interstate, heading toward his dad. Since that time he'd broken his arm, months ago, he'd been e-mailing Dad regularly, and Dad always sounded interested and concerned. Of course, no e-mail or phone calls were allowed at Camp Heritage. He didn't know for sure if his father was even aware of his incarceration there. If he was, what had Mom and Floyd told him?

"Incorrigible. Unmanageable. Disobedient. Insolent. Disrespectful. Mouthy." Those were all words Floyd had used in describing him.

And Marc had kept most of the words bottled up, hadn't voiced them aloud.

He was glad he'd found the lost bungee cord. He couldn't trust Rat not to get too close to the highway; he was too young to have any brains about cars. The cord made it possible for the dog to walk instead of having to be carried, which was a relief to Marc.

He didn't know how long he walked, the dog trotting beside or before him. The trouble with walking against traffic, the way he was supposed to do to be safe, was that if he did spot a K & M truck, it was going the wrong direction. Then again, he didn't know if he could get one to stop even if he tried to flag it down.

He expected that any minute someone would stop him and accuse him of murdering the guard at the camp, but apparently the news hadn't gotten out yet. When a California Highway Patrol black and white roared past, coming from behind, he thought for sure it would slam on the brakes and arrest him. The cop cars all had radios, and Marc had no doubt that they'd know quickly once the alarm was put out. So that hadn't happened yet, if the CHP didn't stop to check out a fourteen-year-old boy wandering along an isolated stretch of I-5.

How long would it be before everybody on the road knew about him? Before one of the staff went out to investigate why he and Stoner and Klammer hadn't returned to camp? Sometimes one of the guards and a few of the boys were gone all day, chopping wood, clearing brush, doing some kind of manufactured labor designed to keep them busy and tired and to never forget they were being disciplined for their sins.

With any kind of luck, the three of them might not be missed until they failed to show up at six to eat. Even then it might be a while before the others found the two bodies, and realized Marc Solie was missing and the probable culprit in one of the deaths.

Nobody could suspect him of Klammer's death. That wouldn't take a genius to figure out, because when Stoner went down under Marc's frantic assault, Klammer was still baking in the intense heat, right out in the sun, with a water bottle deliberately placed just out of his reach. Tied to an iron stake sunk in the red earth, like a goat being used as bait to lure in the hungry coyotes or one of the bears that roamed this area.

Even the stupidest of investigators, Marc thought, would have to realize that the guard, Sergeant Stoner, had put the boy into these restraints and deprived him of water. Wouldn't an autopsy show that Klammer had died of sunstroke?

Unless, of course, Captain Jasper and the other guards rearranged the scene before they called in civilian authorities. If they brought Klammer back to camp and put him on his own cot, and claimed he'd simply succumbed to the heat, and they'd tried to do something for him, could they cover it up? Put a water bottle next to him, say they'd tried to get some into him, and to cool him off?

Would there be telltale marks on his wrists, where he'd been cuffed? Stoner had used regular handcuffs, and it was hot enough that the sun on the metal would have burned him. But badly enough to leave evidence of what had happened to him?

Marc was jerked out of his reverie when, on the opposite side of the road, an old pickup and a small trailer slowed and pulled off onto the shoulder. Whoever it was just sat there, waiting for Marc to come up even. Anybody could have a CB these days; once the word was out, everybody on the West Coast who had a radio could be told to look for a boy in jeans and a T-shirt and athletic shoes, who was wanted by the police.

Marc didn't know whether to be apprehensive or hopeful. Maybe the guy would give him a ride on to the next town, or at least to a rest stop, where he could watch for a K & M truck, going in the right direction. He didn't know if he'd dare approach any other driver, because virtually every truck ran a CB these days. Even a K & M driver might not believe he was their dispatcher's kid, though he could easily find out. Would his being Hank Solie's kid be enough to convince a K & M driver to at least check with the office before turning him over to the authorities?

An old man stuck his head out the window of the pickup. "You lost, sonny? You're a long way from a watering hole."

"You're telling me," Marc agreed, stopping opposite him. "You wouldn't by any chance give me a ride, would you? I'm heading for Seattle, but I'd take a ride anywhere."

"Ain't going anywhere near as far as Seattle," the old man said. His wispy white hair stirred in the hot wind.

"But I can give you a boost as far as the next rest area, if that'll help. Better place to hitch a ride from there. At least the cars will be stopped. Come on, get in."

Marc scooped up Rat, waited for a break in the traffic, and ran across the road and around the back of the trailer. It was a really old one, with California plates. He wondered if the old guy had much to eat in there. They had taken sack lunches out into the woods this morning, but Klammer never got a chance to eat his, and lunch had been the last thing on Marc's mind when he'd fled.

The door of the pickup eased open as he reached it, and he threw Rat up ahead of him, then climbed in. The old man smelled as if it had been a while since he'd had a bath, but Marc couldn't afford to be picky.

"Name's Louie," the driver said. "Louie Esterhausen."

"I'm Marc—" His name was out of his mouth before it occurred to him that he might be safer to make up a new one. "Martin," he improvised. "Marc Martin. This is Rat."

The old man chuckled, then put the truck in gear to let it roll slowly forward until he could safely merge with the intermittent traffic. "Kind of fits him, don't it? He ain't much for looks."

"He's a good dog, though," Marc defended him. "He's had a rough life, but he's my friend."

"Sure. Everybody's had a rough life, one way or another. Dog don't need a pedigree to be a buddy, though. Had me a dog oncet or twicet in my life. All of 'em mongrels." Louie Esterhausen found a spot to pull out, and quickly brought the old truck up to speed.

The pickup had no air-conditioning, but at highway

speed the moving air quickly evaporated the sweat off Marc's face and torso. "I don't suppose you got any water?"

"Sure, got a jug right there by your feet. Won't be cold, but it's wet. Help yourself."

There it was, a gallon jug, half-empty.

"This all you have?" Marc asked, concerned about taking the last of the man's water, but feeling like he could drink all of it, he was so dehydrated.

"No, no, got more in the trailer. Reckon your pooch needs some too. Wait a minute—ought to be a place to pull over before long. I'll go back and get something to pour it into for your Rat." He chuckled again, at the name.

Marc licked his lips. "You got anything to eat back there? That you can spare, I mean. I don't have any money."

"Yeah, I can find something. Give us a few minutes. What you doing out here in the wilderness with no money, boy?"

He'd been thinking frantically, trying to come up with something that sounded credible. "I'm on my way to see my dad, in Seattle. I did have money for a bus ticket, but I lost it somehow. Maybe somebody picked my pocket in the bus station. Anyway, I decided to hitchhike, and when my first ride's car overheated and he had to stop, I decided to walk a ways."

He'd seen cars steaming, hoods up, dead in the water until they could get cooled down.

"Pays to carry water with you over these hills," Louie observed. "Too bad about your money. People ain't as honest as they used to be, seems like. Stealing off a kid like you. Seattle's a long ways off."

"Yeah," Marc agreed, and noticed that there was no sign of a CB. It felt good to be sitting, riding, instead of walking. "How far you going, Mr. Esterhausen?"

"Oh, call me Louie. Esterhausen's a mouthful. I'm only going as far as Castella. Know where that is?"

"No," Marc said. He'd never heard of it.

"Got a sister there. Older'n I am. Eighty-six. I'm only seventy-eight. Reckon you're about sixteen, right?"

"Right," Marc agreed. He could get pretty good at lying if this kept up.

Ten minutes later there was a wide enough spot to pull off the pavement. "Come on back, I could use a snack myself," Louie said, and Marc took Rat with him to the trailer.

It was cramped, but probably not bad for one person, Marc figured. There was a two-burner stove, and a small refrigerator, from which Louie produced a couple of Cokes and a package of lunch meat. He also put a jar of mayonnaise on the table, and a knife to spread it with. They each built their own sandwich. Louie looked at Rat, and ran some water into a pan, and the dog drank it all, plus a refill, before he was satisfied.

"Reckon he'd like some lunch meat too," Louie decided. "You think he wants it in a sandwich, with mayonnaise?"

"I guess he'd about eat anything that didn't eat him first," Marc said, and took a swig of the ice-cold Coke. He didn't know when he'd ever tasted anything so good.

Louie opened an overhead cupboard and brought forth a partially eaten bag of chips, divvying them up between them on a couple of paper towels. "Kind of smashed up," he said, stating the obvious, "but they still taste okay, I guess."

They did. Marc ate ravenously, and so did Rat, who waited patiently after he'd gobbled his sandwich, until Louie took pity on him and made him another. Marc would have liked a second one as well, but he didn't want to ask, and Louie didn't offer. The old man had no way of knowing just how hungry he was.

Louie put what was left of the food away, and they climbed back into the pickup. "Want to get to Harriet's early enough so's she knows I'm staying for supper. Hope she's got some pork chops. She does a mean pork chop," he said. "If she's got some in the freezer, won't take long to defrost 'em in this weather."

When the blue and white sign showed up, Marc read it aloud. "Rest area, one mile."

"Yep. You'll catch a ride from there," Louie predicted, and turned in when they reached it.

There were half a dozen trucks, none of them white with blue trim, and twice as many cars and trailers. There was one of those big Prevo motor homes, painted fancy with gold swirls on black—really classy. Now that would be the way to ride on into Seattle, Marc thought, but knew it wasn't likely they'd offer a ride to a kid with a dog.

Louie went inside to the rest room, and Marc got out with Rat and stood looking around, trying to decide on the possibilities.

He wished he still believed in prayers. He thought they could use some help right about now.

7

Louie came out of the rest room and nodded at the string of vehicles. "You'll catch a ride from here," he assured Marc.

"Sure. Thanks for the ride and the lunch and the water, Louie. I hope your sister cooks the pork chops."

Louie got in the pickup and waved a hand as he pulled out of the rest area. Rat piddled in the grass in the pet area, but Marc wasn't yet rehydrated enough to need to go.

He had lived all his life in Eureka, on the coast, until he was dragged off to Camp Heritage. The first couple of weeks he'd been there he thought he would die from the heat, and Captain Jasper and the rest of the staff made no allowance for "sissies" from more temperate climates. They expected the boys to work hard and long, and they didn't care if the heat made them throw up or pass out or feel as if they couldn't breathe because the air seared their lungs.

While he was standing there, trying to decide if he should approach someone—who?—to ask about a ride, a CHP black and white pulled into the rest area. Marc froze.

It was too late to get out of sight without running, and then he'd be conspicuous. He didn't want to call attention to himself, in case the cop was looking for a boy guilty of taking a life.

The car nosed in to the curb, and a uniformed officer stepped out. He nodded briefly at Marc as he passed and went on into the building. Cops had to relieve themselves the same as everybody else.

If there had been anywhere to retreat to, any shade, Marc would have gotten out of sight. He tugged at the bungee cord and urged Rat into sluggish movement, anywhere so the cop didn't notice him again on the way back to his patrol car. Sooner or later he'd hear that a boy of Marc's description was wanted in connection with what had happened to Stoner, and remember where he'd seen him, so they walked the length of the parking area to get away from him.

A few minutes later the patrol car passed him, heading north, and Marc breathed more easily. He turned around to walk back to the other end of the parking lot.

He passed an overflowing garbage can and stopped. There were two plastic water bottles in the debris around its base. They were empty, but there was a water fountain only a few yards away.

Marc picked up the bottles and carried them to the fountain, where he drank his fill and scrubbed at the dark stains remaining around his fingernails. Then he poured water into an empty cottage cheese carton for Rat. Finally, hoping whoever had discarded the plastic bottles hadn't had any communicable disease, he rinsed the containers out and refilled them from the fountain.

Rat watched him hopefully. When nothing further was forthcoming, the dog began to nose around in the spilled trash, discovering something that he swallowed in a gulp.

"What did you find? Something worthwhile?" Marc asked. He stepped aside when an overweight woman in short shorts got out of a red Toyota and paused to empty her trash on top of the rest of the pile.

There was a paper tray with a few French fries that Rat quickly gobbled up. The woman went on toward the building, and Marc stuck out a foot and wriggled it through the rest of the junk, hoping there might be something else edible there.

There wasn't, but a few minutes later he heard a man say, "For crying out loud, Jeremy, why did you ask for a hamburger if you weren't going to eat it?"

"I didn't want mustard on it," the little boy whined, and the father disgustedly tossed the still-wrapped burger right in front of Marc.

Marc liked mustard just fine. He waited until the family went on past, then snatched it up. It not only had catsup and mustard, it had cheese. Only one bite had been taken out of it, and Marc's mouth watered.

He wasn't starving yet, thanks to the sandwich Louie had given him, but he'd sure save it for later. He found an empty plastic bag big enough to hold both the burger and the water bottles—as an afterthought he added the empty cheese carton for Rat's water dish—and knotted the top of the bag so that it hung down from his belt and banged against his behind. It was awkward, but he felt better having it.

He had a sudden understanding of what homeless

people must endure, pawing through Dumpsters, retrieving odds and ends to keep from starving. His heart thumped so hard that he felt it. Homeless people. He was essentially homeless now too, until he could reach Dad.

A big green SUV pulled in alongside him, and a man got out. He had lots of room in his vehicle. Marc eyed him speculatively, waiting until he returned from the rest room before speaking to him.

"Sir, any chance you could give me a lift north? I'm heading for Seattle."

The man didn't even pause. "Forget it, kid. Nobody but an idiot picks up hitchhikers these days." He stepped off the curb, opened his car door, and hesitated. "Even innocent-looking kids'll stick a knife in your back for your rig."

"I don't have a knife," Marc said, but the guy had already slammed the door and turned on the ignition.

Louie hadn't been afraid to pick him up. Of course, he hadn't been driving a forty-thousand-dollar SUV. Maybe, Marc figured, he'd have better luck if he tried someone else driving an older vehicle, something not so valuable.

There weren't many vehicles that fit that description. The elegant Prevo pulled out and another SUV took its place, but it was loaded with teenagers, all laughing and shoving one another as they got out.

No room there. Nor in the next two cars, each of which was carrying two couples.

The next rig to pull in was a rusty old Chevy pickup pulling an empty horse trailer. A big German shepherd stuck his head out the passenger-side window. Another truck without air-conditioning, but better than walking, if the driver was receptive.

To Marc's surprise, the driver was a girl. Well, a young woman. She wore jeans and a western-style plaid shirt, and well-worn boots.

She noticed Marc staring at her and smiled as she passed. His heartbeat quickened. Yes, when she came back, he'd confront her. Ask for a ride.

His tongue felt almost stuck in his mouth, and he ducked his head over the fountain and drank as much as he could hold. Then instead of getting out the cottage cheese carton for Rat, he lifted him and let him lap out of the fountain itself.

"Glad I don't have to do that with Mikey," a feminine voice said, and he looked up into the face of the girl from the rusty pickup. "He weighs over a hundred pounds."

"Rat's not very heavy," Marc said. He almost chickened out, dreading another response like the one from the green SUV driver. But desperation lent him courage.

"Uh—I don't suppose you could give us a lift, could you? Going north?"

She studied him carefully. He could see rejection forming in her mind. After all, if a full-grown man was afraid to pick him up, what could he expect of a girl traveling alone?

"I'm not going very far," the girl said. "Only into Yreka. Where you going?"

"Seattle. But I'll take a ride as far as I can get."

"Okay. Let me water Mikey first." She reached into the bed of the truck and got out a battered stainless steel bowl, which she filled at the fountain and held in the window for her dog to drink.

"Uh—he won't eat Rat if we get in, will he?"

She laughed. "No way. Not unless I tell him to."

"Thanks for taking a chance on me. Some drivers won't pick up anybody."

"You're not packing, unless you're better at hiding a weapon than I think you are. And Mikey is very protective. If I tell him to kill you, he will."

Looking at the massive head in the truck window, Marc believed her. "I can hold Rat on my lap," he offered, knowing it might be kind of crowded in the cab with two people and two dogs.

"Sure. Move over, Mikey. We've got company."

The shepherd didn't move until she shoved him over into the middle. She reached out for Rat. "I'll hold him while you get in."

Mikey smelled like dog, and he emanated warmth, but at least Marc would be riding. He reached out and detached the plastic bag so he wouldn't be sitting on his hamburger and the water bottles. He set it at his feet, and took Rat onto his lap.

Mikey leaned over and started sniffing Rat. Marc braced himself, but the girl said, "No, Mikey. Leave him alone," and to Marc's relief the big dog obeyed.

"My name's Jenny. What's yours?" the girl asked as she got into the driver's seat and turned the key.

"Marc. You live around here?"

"In the hills back of Yreka. My dad has a ranch there. Where'd your dog get a name like Rat?"

"He looked like one when he was a puppy."

"He still does, kind of," Jenny said, and they both laughed.

It felt good to be moving. The hot air still parched his lungs, and he knew he'd never come back to this country again if he ever successfully got out of it. With Rat in his lap and Mikey pressed against his side, Marc thought longingly of being back in Eureka, with cool breezes coming off the ocean, and a home with a filled refrigerator and all the water he wanted to drink, and a lukewarm shower. Once he got his belly completely filled, the shower would be the most tempting thing of all.

Jenny reached out and turned on the radio, and for a moment Marc tensed, expecting a CB, but it was only a regular radio. It was tuned to a country western station, and he recognized the voice of Waylon Jennings.

He was glad Jenny chose music over conversation—it would be too hard to answer questions if she asked them. He didn't want to make up a bunch of lies. In spite of the number of falsehoods he'd been obliged to produce lately, he was basically truthful and he preferred to stay that way. Though with all he'd been through these past few weeks, and especially this morning, lying seemed a pretty small crime.

Rat settled down, closing his eyes. It wasn't long before Marc began to nod off as well. Jenny was a good driver, taking the frequent curves of the road expertly, singing under her breath along with the radio.

He drifted into a semidoze, finally relaxing with the sway of the truck. He was exhausted, worn out from climbing the hills and worrying about pursuit and succumbing to terror.

The fear retreated as sleep dragged him under, and the dreams took over. For a while they were good dreams—kind of stupid, the way dreams usually are, with no plot—of the days before Mallory got sick.

They'd been a great family then. They'd done things together, and laughed a lot, and had fun. And then, all of a sudden, Stoner was standing over him, and Marc knew the man intended to beat him within an inch of his life. To kill him. Not the way he'd killed Klammer, but brutally, with his fists and his whip. The guys had talked about what Stoner could do with that whip, and there'd been universal agreement that if he took that whip to any of them they'd fight back, the best they could.

Marc lived through the whole thing again, and it was even worse in the dream than it had been in actuality. Breathing hard, his blood racing, he woke with a jerk, almost sending Rat onto the floor.

It wasn't possible that the dream was true . . . but it was, and the nightmare wouldn't go away just because he woke up. He glanced at Jenny, and was relieved to see she hadn't noticed. Now she was singing along with George Jones, unaware of her passenger.

Mikey was aware that something had transpired. He turned his head and licked at Marc's ear, as if in sympathy.

Dad had always told him that it was a waste of time to feel sorry for himself. That was undoubtedly true, but

Marc wondered how many people, even Dad, would be unable to resist self-pity under these circumstances.

He stared again through the dirty windshield, seeing the steep red banks on the west side of the highway, the guardrail and treetops far below on the east, and occasionally a glimpse of a river—the Sacramento?—even farther down.

Every mile took him farther from Camp Heritage and Captain Jasper and the nightmare that had been all too real.

But Marc knew with certainty that eventually it would all catch up with him.

8

"Uh-oh," Jenny said. "Something must be up. There's a Chippie right behind me, moving well over the speed limit and with his lights flashing. I'm right at the speed I want, so he can't be after me."

She eased up on the gas and cut over to the extreme right to get out of the way. There was no shoulder. Only a few feet of space separated the fog line from a guardrail on the edge of a steep embankment, with treetops below the road level.

"Chippie" was how Californians often referred to their highway patrol officers. Panic clogged Marc's chest. He expected to be hauled out of the stopped pickup by the front of his shirt and thrown bodily into the rear of the patrol car.

Ahead of them several other vehicles pulled over as well, and a moment later the black and white swept past them, red and blue lights blinking frantically, to disappear quickly around the next curve.

Almost in shock, Marc sucked in a breath, unable to believe the cop had gone on by. Had he been looking for a juvenile delinquent and merely missed seeing him in the pickup, the driver and the big dog blocking his view?

Jenny hadn't noticed his agitation. "Probably a wreck up ahead," she said, pulling back into traffic with the others and gradually picking up speed. "People tend to take these corners too fast in spite of all the signs that tell you what's safe."

"Safe," Marc muttered, scarcely able to think. Well, it seemed he was safe for the moment. Though if the officer had been looking for him, the danger was not over, only postponed.

Gradually the tumult in his chest subsided. He didn't. fall asleep again, but he started wondering about where he would sleep tonight if he couldn't get another ride after Jenny dropped him off in Yreka.

It wasn't a very big town, from what he remembered. He suspected they rolled up the sidewalks and locked all the doors shortly after dark, which came early, with mountains rising to the west to cut off the sun long before it dropped below the horizon.

In spite of the extreme heat during the day, the temperature dropped sharply at night. He'd had a jacket early this morning when he left camp, but he'd discarded it somewhere hours ago, long before the confrontation with Stoner.

He didn't want to think about Stoner right now. The entire episode was so depressing, and he couldn't take any of it back. It was already done. He didn't even know for sure if he'd take it back if he could, not if Stoner had come on the same way.

He tried to think about more pleasant things, but all the really good stuff had happened such a long time ago. Without wanting to, Marc recalled the last few months of his life before he'd come to Camp Heritage.

Matters at home had gone from bad to worse.

In spite of the fact that the insurance business with Marc's mom must have been concluded a long time ago, Floyd kept coming around. Frequently he was there for dinner, and afterward he sat around watching TV, with his feet up on the coffee table. That was a habit Mom had always deplored when Marc did it, but she never said a word to Floyd.

The man started bringing his kids around too. Barbara was fifteen, sort of lanky and quite plain except for remarkable hazel eyes. Annette, the younger daughter, was twelve, and had more freckles than anybody else Marc had ever seen.

When they were introduced, Marc shuffled his feet uncomfortably, and the girls stared at him as if he were a freak. What had Floyd said about him? he wondered.

Nobody even noticed when he had his fourteenth birthday. He kept thinking surely Mom would bake him a cake, at least, but she was busy painting the kitchen and never mentioned it. Dad's card came the following day, a day late, and had twenty-five-dollar check in it. His note was brief.

"Having a few problems here, buddy; things have come up I have to take care of. On top of everything else, my computer crashed, so I don't even have e-mail right now. But I love you and will be in touch. Have a great birthday!"

Sure, Marc thought sourly. *All by myself.*

He showed the check to his mom, thinking she'd be apologetic because she hadn't remembered. All she said was, "Good. You can save it for your school clothes in the fall."

School clothes? Who wanted to spend their birthday money on jeans and Nikes?

Marc got used to seeing the blue Caddie in the driveway. But it took him by surprise when one day he walked into his bedroom and found Barbara and Annette there, playing games on his computer.

He went ballistic.

"Hey! What do you think you're doing? That's my personal computer! The stuff on it is private!"

The girls turned away from the screen. "We didn't open any of your documents," Barbara said. "Your mom said we could play games."

His mother appeared in the hallway behind him. "Marc, where are your manners? The girls are guests, and they're not hurting a thing!"

He knew the color had faded out of his face, and his anger held. "You had no right to let them into my room. To let them use my PC."

"I'm ashamed of you, Marc," his mother said. She must be painting something upstairs now, because there were yellow smears on her shirt and jeans.

Furious, feeling cheated and imposed on, Marc snapped back, "And I'm ashamed of you! You used to have a sense of privacy, and you expected me to have one too!"

Floyd materialized out of the bathroom, holding a paintbrush. "I expect you to show more respect than that, young man, when you speak to your mother."

"Who cares what you expect?" The rage boiled out of him, crushing his common sense. "You're not a member of this family, so we don't need your opinion!"

"Marc!" Mom turned a chagrined face toward Floyd. "I'm sorry, I don't know what's gotten into him."

"Maybe it's time we told him," Floyd said. "I don't intend to go on overlooking his rude behavior."

"Told me what?" Marc demanded, suddenly apprehensive.

"Floyd, please, we haven't decided anything—"

"Patricia, you're letting this brat run our lives into the ground. There's no reason to tolerate it. If you don't want to deal with him, I'll be happy to."

The anger flooded through him again, mingled now with fear—because Mom wasn't objecting to having him called a brat, but was instead trying to placate Floyd.

Floyd stepped inside Marc's bedroom to speak to his daughters. "If he doesn't want you using his computer, shut it down, girls. We'll be leaving in a few minutes anyway, as soon as we clean up our painting stuff." He swiveled slightly to face Marc. "As for you, I warn you now to watch your mouth, or I promise you'll be sorry. I've asked your mother to marry me, and I refuse to put up with insubordination in my own household."

He didn't know why he hadn't anticipated something like this, but he hadn't. The idea was so repugnant, so disgusting, that Marc was barely able to make it to the freshly painted yellow bathroom before he threw up.

Behind him, he heard Barbara speaking in a low but clear voice. "Thanks a lot, Daddy. You've just made it pretty well impossible for us ever to be a family in this house. He's never going to be civil to any of us, ever."

Floyd didn't give an inch. "He'll be civil, I promise you. Come on, help us carry these paint cans downstairs."

In the bathroom on his knees, Marc squeezed his eyes shut against the hot tears.

It couldn't be true. Mom couldn't marry the guy, could she? Floyd couldn't become his stepfather, those stupid girls his stepsisters!

Long after they'd left, and as his mother sat reading in the living room, Marc emerged from his room and went downstairs. He stood in the dim light, waiting until she looked up.

"Is it true? Are you going to marry him?"

She marked her place in the book with a finger. "Marc, I didn't want you to hear it that way. We're talking about it. We've become friends, and we both need someone—a mate—in our lives. You know why I can't bring myself to sell this house, though it's true I can't really afford to keep it: It holds everything I have left of Mallory. But Floyd has suggested that he sell his place and they move in with us. His girls need a mother, and you need a father. . . ."

He'd thought he had calmed down, that he could talk to her. But the outrage was impossible to contain. For the first time in his life, he yelled at her. "Not him! Mom, there's no way I can live with him as a stepfather! He hates me! Can't you see that? He hates me, and I hate him!"

"You haven't even tried to get to know him, Marc.

He's kind, considerate. And he understands about Mallory's things, how I can't give them up. Please, son, try to see this from my point of view. I'm a woman alone, with a son to raise—"

"Then let me go live with Dad!"

"Marc—" She hesitated, biting her lip. "Your father has never offered to take you."

"He never said he didn't want me! Did he? Did he?"

"No," Mom said finally. "Marc, give this some time. We thought you'd be better off here, in your old school, than going off to a strange place."

"So how come I don't get any say about it? What if I don't care where I go to school? I don't care if I never go back to my old school! You ignored my birthday, and let those girls into my bedroom, and I've got private stuff on the computer, Mom! It's not for just anybody to get into!"

"I'm sure they didn't get into anything but the games, and what could that hurt? Please, son, you're grown up enough to understand that we can't always have things the way we want them to be—"

He turned away in a violent movement and ran back up the stairs. When she rose to follow him a few steps, he hollered at her, "I wish I was dead! And I wish you were too!"

He knew she was crying, and he managed not to care about that, either. But he wouldn't cry. He didn't care enough about anything to cry about it.

He wanted to talk to Dad, but there was no e-mail and he didn't dare call him—Mom would have a fit if he added anything to the long-distance bills.

I'll ask him if I can go live with him and Grandma Belle, he thought. He couldn't live in this house if Floyd and his daughters moved in with them. *Surely if I ask him outright, he'll let me go up to Seattle.*

But though he checked every day—even several times a day—there was no e-mail. There were no phone calls from Seattle. What kind of problems could Dad be dealing with that he couldn't at least call?

And then, with no such intention, he cooked his goose with Floyd.

He'd been over at Toby's house, playing computer games. Anything to take his mind off the things he couldn't control, which was his entire life, practically.

He knew he was late, and it was starting to rain hard as he approached home. The blue Caddie was there in the driveway, and Marc had no doubt Floyd would have something to say about his missing dinner. Even though he was sure Floyd didn't really care if he ever ate another meal.

He was already soaked, so he couldn't have said why he tried to take a shortcut across the wet lawn. The tires of his bike skidded when he hit the brakes, and he knew within seconds that he was going to crash into the Caddie.

He put down his feet, trying to stop, but it didn't do any good. He jerked the handlebars of his bike sharply to the left, hoping to deflect the impact, and smashed right into that blue, polished door.

He forgot the rain pouring down on him as he stared at the damage. The words that spilled out of his mouth were profane and appropriate, but did nothing to help the situation.

He had scraped his bike basket in a horrible smear across the driver's door, taking the paint with it.

For a moment he literally couldn't breathe.

Floyd loved this car. And he couldn't stand Marc. *Oh, God, open up the earth and swallow me!*

Then he remembered he wasn't speaking to God, and God certainly wasn't speaking to him.

He knew, instinctively, that the honorable thing to do was go inside and confess. Maybe Floyd would believe it had been an accident. He'd still be livid, but maybe he wouldn't want to kill him.

On the other hand, it was late. It could well be full dark before Floyd left. Maybe he wouldn't notice the damage until tomorrow, and he might think somebody'd nicked him in a parking lot. He might never find out that Marc had been the culprit.

He put his bike into the garage and let himself in through the kitchen door. His plate was still on the table, though the food had been put away. He couldn't have eaten anything if his life had depended on it.

Voices emanated from the dining room, and laughter. It was Floyd and Barbara and Annette, playing some board game.

He had to go through the dining room to get to the stairs that led to the sanctuary of his own room. His shoes were squishing, and he took them off and left them by the back door, walking in wet socks toward the voices.

Monopoly. How many times had he and his parents

and Mallory sat around that same table, playing games that made them laugh? How could his mother now be participating with them, as if they were a new and better family?

Barbara looked around at him, the only one to speak. "We're just finishing a game, if you want to play the next one."

"No thanks," Marc said. He expected a tirade against his lateness, but there was none. He went on through the dining area and up to his room, where he checked to see if there was any new e-mail.

Nothing.

Dad, please call! Please tell me what to do! Telepathy had never worked for him before, but maybe his sheer desperation would get through.

He waited, sitting alone in the darkening room, for Floyd to leave. He heard the murmur of voices, and the front door close, and strained to hear the engine starting. And then the door opened again, and the bellow of Floyd's wrath rose up to meet him.

Marc sat with his eyes closed, in the dark, waiting for the axe to fall.

9

There was blue paint on the basket of his bike.

He could hardly deny anything. He should have followed through on his initial impulse to walk into the house and admit his guilt and take his punishment.

Not that it would have alleviated any of Floyd's fury.

"Do you have any idea what it will cost to fix that?"

Marc had never particularly noticed Floyd's eyes before, but now they bulged, a pale blue and so malevolent that he wouldn't have been surprised if the man had physically attacked him.

"It was an accident," Marc said, dry-mouthed. "I slid on the wet grass. I tried to stop, but I couldn't."

"If you'd come home when you were supposed to, you wouldn't have been in such a hurry." Floyd's chest rose and fell in his agitation. His fists were clenched at his sides. They were bigger fists than Marc might have thought.

"Floyd, I'll pay for the repairs," Mom said, distressed.

"Is that the way you mean to go on for the rest of his life? Paying for the stupid things he does? They may have to repaint the entire car to get it to match! It'll cost a fortune!"

In some small corner of his brain Marc denied that it would be necessary to repaint the whole car; he'd seen doors repainted to match before. But he was too frozen to respond to the exaggeration.

"I'm sure it really was an accident," Mom said, her hands clutched together at her breast. "Please, listen to him!"

But what was there to say? He'd already said it. Marc huddled miserably in his chair, facing them.

"If there wasn't a law against it," Floyd stated in a low, deadly tone, "I'd strangle you right this minute."

There was more, but Marc stayed mute, trying not to hear the rest of it. Finally they left him alone.

He didn't even bother to get undressed or go to bed. He sat there in his room, wallowing in his misery. How had he come to this point? What could he possibly do to extricate himself from what seemed the depths of hell?

Around midnight, sleepless, he went downstairs and out to the garage. Sure enough, there was blue paint on his bike, not just on the basket. No wonder there was so much damage to the car.

Marc stared at it mournfully. From somewhere came the impulse to destroy the evidence, though Floyd had already seen it. He pulled out his jackknife and scraped away at the telltale blue paint, leaving scratch marks on the bike itself.

So what? It was his bike.

He went back upstairs and sat at his desk, finally leaning forward on his arms, too spent to even go into the bathroom and get a couple of aspirins for his headache. He hadn't eaten anything since lunch yesterday, but he didn't think he could swallow, let alone keep anything down.

At six thirty he jerked awake when his mother came to the doorway. "Time to get up, Marc. Oh, you are dressed. Well, come down and eat. I've made oatmeal."

He hated oatmeal. How could she have lived with him in the same house for fourteen years and not yet figured out he hated oatmeal?

"I didn't get any sleep. I'm not going to school," he said.

"Of course you're going to school. I know you're feeling bad, but the best thing is to get back into your normal routine as quickly as possible. Honey, Floyd's a reasonable man. A good man. He's angry now, but he'll get over it. I'm sure he realizes that it really was an accident."

Marc stared at her helplessly. "He didn't like me before—he's never going to tolerate me now. You're not really going to marry him, are you? Have him move in with us here?"

"Marc, this isn't the time to discuss it. Come down and eat, and go on to school. Things will work out."

He didn't see how, but he was too beat to argue. He went downstairs and ate the oatmeal, made marginally palatable with brown sugar and raisins, and two slices of whole wheat toast loaded with apricot jam. It wasn't enough to make him feel normal, but it was easier than fighting with his mother again.

He met Toby on the way to school and told him what had happened.

Aghast, Toby tripped over his shoestrings. "You didn't! Holy cow, Marc, I'm surprised you lived through the night!"

"Yeah. Tobe, how am I going to dig myself out of this hole? And if Mom marries him, he'll be right there in the house with us."

Toby licked his lips. "Pray?" he suggested doubtfully.

"I don't remember the last time one of my prayers was answered. I don't bother anymore."

"Your dad sends child support money, doesn't he?"

"Yeah, I guess."

"Well, maybe—maybe I could talk to my folks. They like you, Marc. You're their favorite of all my friends. Maybe if your dad sent the money to them, they'd let you come and live with us. When I tell them what you're going through. They felt real bad about Mallory, and then about the divorce—I know they feel sorry for you."

Having somebody feel sorry for him wasn't exactly what he wanted, but Marc couldn't help being a trace hopeful, though it seemed a long shot.

"You really think they might buy it?"

"I can ask. This is Dad's bowling night, so he won't be home, but I can sound out Mom and she'll talk to him later. Okay?"

"Okay," Marc said, not quite daring to hope, but unable to resist entirely.

The morning went reasonably well. They had a quiz in math, which he aced, and then an assembly, so he didn't have to worry about what happened during that time period.

And then at lunchtime it all fell apart.

He was eating with Toby and a couple of other guys in the cafeteria. Toby had a carton of milk that refused to open the way it was supposed to; it was tearing without letting him at the contents. He scowled at it. "Man, they sure make crummy stuff these days. How am I supposed to get into this sucker?"

"Poke a hole in it," Joe Smathers suggested.

"With what? These lousy dull knives won't cut through soft butter," Toby muttered.

"Here. This'll cut it." Marc pulled out the jackknife he'd never taken out of his pocket after scraping the paint off his bike.

"Yeah! Right," Toby said, and stabbed at the cardboard carton.

A moment later an ominous voice said, "What do you mean, bringing a knife to school? That's strictly against the rules, Tobin."

Toby looked up, stricken. "Oh—yeah. Uh, it's not my knife."

The lunchroom monitor looked grim. "This is a reportable offense, you know."

Marc ought to have been getting used to having his mouth go dry—it was happening often enough. "Uh—," he managed, "it's my knife. We were just using it to get into Toby's milk carton. You can see it tore without opening."

"We have a no-tolerance policy against weapons of any kind," the monitor said. He sounded as if he'd just discovered a body in Marc's locker.

"It isn't a weapon. It's just a jackknife. My dad gave it to me for my twelfth birthday. I was using it last night and forgot to take it out of my pocket this morning."

"You're Solie, right? Marc Solie. I'm going to have to report this." He held out a hand, palm open. "And confiscate the knife."

Toby glanced at Marc, then laid the closed knife in the man's hand.

"I think you'd better come to the office with me," the monitor said, and after a momentary hesitation, Marc rose to his feet.

"We were just using it to open a milk carton. We didn't hurt anything."

There was no response from the monitor as Marc was herded out of the lunchroom, the object of dozens of stares. Toby gazed after them woefully.

Of course, they called Marc's mother.

He sat in the outer office until she got there, out of breath from hurrying, alarm written on her face.

"Marc, what happened?"

"I used the knife late last night and forgot to leave it home this morning," Marc said, having little hope that anything he said would help matters.

"Mrs. Solie," the principal said, suggesting imminent doom, "we absolutely have no tolerance for a weapon of any kind. All our students are aware of that policy."

"Weapon?" Mom echoed. "But it's only a jackknife! My husband gave it to him for his birthday a couple of years ago. Hank always carries a jackknife. He thought Marc was old enough to carry one too."

"Not to school. A jackknife is definitely a weapon, Mrs. Solie. You realize I've had to report this to the authorities."

"Authorities?" Mom sounded faint. "You mean—the police? You can't be serious, Mr. Tustin!"

"I've never been more serious, Mrs. Solie. You remember the incident last year when a student brought a gun to school—"

"But that was a loaded gun! This is only a jackknife!"

"Any type of knife at all is absolutely forbidden. You may both wait in my office until the police arrive," he said. And though Marc had always thought the man to be reasonable and fair, there was no humor in him now.

They didn't have to wait long. The uniformed officer arrived, looking equally stern, and asked a lot of questions. There must have been a reason why Marc brought the knife to school. What did he intend to do with it?

"Nothing," Marc insisted. "I just forgot to take it out of my pocket after I scraped the paint off my bike."

A frown formed on the officer's face. "And why were you scraping paint off your bike?"

He shouldn't have said that. They weren't going to stop now until they learned about the problem with Floyd's car. "It was an accident. My bike skidded on the wet grass, and I couldn't stop. I scratched his car door."

"And you scraped paint off the door of this Cadillac?"

Marc couldn't immediately reply, his heart was hammering so. His mother responded.

"The car belongs to my friend, Floyd Dunning."

The officer shifted position in his chair. "And how did Mr. Dunning react to this?"

Mom swallowed. "He was angry. But he'll get over it."

"But Marc was angry too, right? At getting caught?

And maybe still angry when he brought the knife to school today? What did you plan to do with it, Marc?"

Frustration flooded through him. What could he say that anyone would listen to, believe? "I didn't plan to do *anything* with it. I forgot it was in my pocket."

"You knew about the no-tolerance policy on weapons, didn't you?"

"Yes. Only I forgot about it. I didn't bring it to do anything!"

"All boys carry jackknives," Mom said earnestly. "They aren't a threat to anyone."

"Not these days, they don't," the officer said. "Schools have had too many incidents of violence to ignore something like this. Perhaps your father can make you understand how seriously we take this kind of thing."

"My husband's in Seattle," Mom said. "We're divorced."

"I see. Well, what will it take to convince you, Marc, of how severely we have to view this?"

"I understand. It was just a mistake. An oversight. I didn't intend to do anything with the knife," Marc said helplessly. "A stupid mistake."

"You make mistakes a lot, do you, Marc?"

He glanced at his mother. "I don't know. No more than anybody else, I guess. Doesn't everybody make mistakes?"

"Marc's a good boy," Mom said. "Things have been difficult for him—for our family—over the past two years. We lost our young daughter to leukemia, and then my husband and I separated and divorced. That's been hard on him. But he hasn't gotten into trouble. He didn't mean to cause any trouble now. I can have the knife back, can't I? It's perfectly legitimate to have a jackknife, away from school."

"You'll have to talk to Mr. Tustin about that. He can't hand it back to Marc."

"He can hand it to me. I assure you, nothing like this will ever happen again."

"It's up to the school how they punish him. They may suspend him," the officer told them.

"Suspend him? What good is that going to do, to cause him to miss school? You mean permanently, or for a few days?"

"That's up to Mr. Tustin," the officer said, and closed his little notebook. "I hope," he said, looking directly at Marc, "that I won't be called back to speak to you about anything more like this."

Marc supposed he ought to say, *No, sir,* but the words were locked in his throat. It was so unfair. He wished his dad were there to back him up, to explain that it had only been a mistake, not a deliberate breaking of the rules. Dad knew why a guy felt the need to carry a jackknife, an all-purpose tool for lots of things.

There was a brisk, though brief, discussion between Mom and the principal about the return of the jackknife. Mom won, and put the offending object into her purse. Her color was now high; her own resentment had risen.

"You will be suspended for three days, Marc," Mr. Tustin stated. "You may return to school on Monday."

Marc had the urge to say that he didn't want to return, ever, but he had sense—and control—enough to resist it. He knew it was impossible for his blood to be boiling, but he felt as if it were.

As he might have guessed, Floyd already knew about the incident at school when he came over that evening. He had a friend on the police department who had relayed the news.

"What is it with you?" he demanded of Marc almost as soon as he walked through the door. "Why can't you stay out of trouble?"

"It was no big deal—," Marc began, but Floyd cut him off harshly.

"What you need, boy, is an attitude adjustment, and I'm beginning to think of ways to bring that about."

What did that mean? Marc looked at his mother, who put a placating hand on Floyd's arm, but said nothing helpful. "It's over now, Floyd. Let's let it drop."

"Until next time? What's he going to do next time? Patricia, are my daughters going to be safe in this house?"

Mom was shocked. "Floyd, that's not fair! Marc has never posed any threat to your daughters! Or to anyone else, for that matter. Maybe we'd all benefit from talking to a counselor, clearing the air—"

Oh, great! She wouldn't consider a counselor when Dad wanted to, to save our family, to keep from getting a divorce. But now she's willing, because Floyd was pressuring her to do something about him. Marc wondered if he'd just smother to death under all of this, and didn't even think he'd care, if it would put an end to the despair.

"Oh," Floyd said, "the air is perfectly clear, my dear. Or it would be if your son would stop poisoning the atmosphere. Don't be upset. I promise you I'll take care of everything. Just leave it to me."

And that, Marc reflected bleakly, was just what he was afraid of. If there was one thing he was sure of, it was that he couldn't expect any mercy from this man who so obviously despised him.

10

For a week nothing happened, and it made Marc nervous.

He returned to school, falling into step with Toby, who was uncharacteristically sober.

Marc didn't really have any hope, now, but he finally had to ask. "Did you talk to your folks?"

Toby grunted assent. Then he said. "Yeah. Only by then everybody in town knew you'd been suspended for taking a knife to school. I told them how it happened, that you'd only loaned it to me to open a stupid carton of milk. That you only had it because you forgot to take it out of your pocket."

"Didn't they believe you?"

"Yeah, I think they did. And they still like you, Marc. But they don't think it would be wise for them to take on responsibility for you. 'For another adolescent male,' Dad said. Implying, I guess, that I'm enough of a handful."

"Did they hear about what happened to Floyd's car?"

Toby sighed. "Yeah. That story got around too." He hesitated. "They feel bad about what's been happening to you, but they think maybe you're . . . disturbed."

"Disturbed!" Marc felt a chill run through him. "Crazy, you mean?"

"No, no. Mom said it was no wonder you were disturbed—upset—losing Mallory and then your folks getting a divorce and your dad leaving town. Nobody thinks you're certifiable or anything like that."

The chill remained, making him hunch his shoulders inside his school jacket. "Except maybe Floyd."

Toby had used the words first, but now he was shaken. "You aren't serious, are you? Cripes, Marc, even if he doesn't like you very much—"

"That's an understatement."

"What can he do about it? You can't lock a kid up because he accidentally runs into your car and forgets he's got a jackknife in his pocket! Can you?"

"I don't know," Marc said slowly. "But I don't trust him. He told Mom he'd 'take care of me.'"

"But he has no legal authority over you. He can't make you do anything." It sounded more like a hope than a fact.

Marc moistened his lips. "He and Mom are talking about getting married. That would make him my stepfather. That might make a difference."

Neither of them knew for sure. And while Toby's parents empathized, it was clear they weren't going to intervene.

The other kids gave him sly or knowing looks when he went back to classes. A few of them made remarks, which he tried to ignore. In fact, he did his best to blend into the walls, making no waves, creating no problems, minding his own business, and not volunteering with answers.

At home, he kept to his room except at mealtimes, doing homework or playing around on the computer. He kept trying Dad's e-mail, and it all came back: The address was not available. For a couple of days Floyd didn't appear, but Marc knew better than to think it was a permanent disappearance.

On Friday of that week, Floyd came to supper. He greeted Mom, and said nothing to Marc. But over a roast and braised potatoes and vegetables, Floyd looked at him. There was a strange little half-smile on his face, as if he knew something Marc didn't.

If it was calculated to be unnerving, it succeeded.

Mom didn't seem to notice anything amiss, but Marc could feel the hostile emanations from the man, and the sense of triumph Floyd was feeling was too evident for him to ignore.

He'd decided something; he'd taken some step. Whatever it was, Marc knew he wasn't going to like it.

He excused himself and took his pie upstairs with him, knowing it would stick in his throat if he tried to eat it sitting under Floyd's gaze.

He finally came downstairs, after nine, thinking the man had left, only to hear the murmur of voices from the living room—soft voices, the kind not intended to carry.

Marc was in his socks, and he padded toward the doorway, anxiety rising in spite of himself. He paused, just out of sight, to listen.

"I investigated this thoroughly, Patricia. I'm assured we can trust these people. I've talked to them on the phone, and I'm impressed with their reputation. It would solve a lot of problems, honey."

It was the first time Marc had heard him use that endearment. That's what Dad had usually called her, and it seemed profane, almost dirty, that someone else should address her that way. He hoped his mother would object, but she didn't. At least not about the affectionate pet name.

At first her voice was so low Marc couldn't make out the words, and then he heard, "I don't think I'm ready to do anything so drastic. He's still upset—over Mallory, over the divorce—but he's always been a good boy, Floyd."

So they were talking about him. Marc held his breath, determined to hear everything he could.

"Sweetheart, you haven't been listening to me. I know he's your son, and you love him. Do you think I don't understand loving your child? Do you think I don't have any compassion for a child who's become troubled and unstable? But we have to consider the rest of the family as well as the boy himself. There are professionals who know more about things like this than we do. There's nothing wrong with taking their advice."

"I don't know. I can't bring myself to agree to it, Floyd."

"Well," Floyd said, sounding as satisfied as if he'd already won her over to whatever he was proposing, "you sleep on it. We'll talk more later."

"I can't sleep," Mom said. "I'm exhausted, but I'm so upset I can't really rest."

"Why don't you talk to the doctor, maybe get some sleeping pills? Under the circumstances, I'm sure he'd be cooperative."

"I don't believe in sleeping pills. I don't believe in taking drugs to make me feel better. It doesn't really solve anything, it just makes my head fuzzy so I can't cope with even ordinary things." She sounded so tired that Marc could have felt sorry for her, if she hadn't been so obviously plotting against him.

Hang in there, Mom. Don't let him talk you into something horrible. Because it *was* horrible—Marc was certain of that.

"All right, whatever you think best. How about a glass of hot milk before you turn in?"

"A glass of hot milk would turn my stomach inside out. It gags me just thinking about it," Mom said, with a trace of her old firmness.

"Okay. How about cocoa? That'll work just as well, and taste better. I'll call you tomorrow, all right? I have to go to Barbara's concert tomorrow night—are you sure you won't go with me to that?"

"No, I don't think so. I couldn't relax enough to enjoy it."

"Well, I don't want to pressure you, honey."

What a lie that was!

"I appreciate that. Hank was always after me—to go back to church, to clear out Mallory's room, to go for counseling—always pushing me, pushing me, until I thought I'd go out of my mind. Please, let me work this out on my own. I have to think of Marc."

"Of course. We both do. And when you've thought it through, we'll do what's necessary. Remember, I'm right beside you, Patricia. You can lean on me. You can trust me to take care of this so that we can go on with our lives together. Now, I'm going on home; I feel guilty leaving the girls alone so much. Barbara's perfectly competent, but they've already been deprived of one parent, I don't want them to handle too much on their own. Walk me to the door and kiss me good night, all right?"

Marc detected the small sounds as they stood up, and he moved quickly back onto the stairs, into the deeper shadows. Watching them exchange a caress at the door made him want to throw up, to scream and yell that Floyd had no right to treat her this way.

He'd forgotten he'd come downstairs for a snack, but now eating was the furthest thing from his mind. Making no sounds, he made his way to his room and closed the door behind him, sinking onto his bed as if he'd been slugged in the belly and knocked off his feet.

All the words Floyd had used were alarming. Floyd's little half-smile at the dinner table, the smarmy way he kept talking to Mom, practically made Marc's blood run cold. He'd heard that phrase all his life, but he'd never felt it before.

What had Floyd investigated? What people? Was he talking about counseling of some kind? How could anyone force him to cooperate with a counselor? Could such a person actually help him, if he decided it was worthwhile to work with any counselor that Floyd had picked out?

But that didn't fit with Floyd's sly smile. Why would he get such satisfaction from that? No, it had to be something more. Floyd was planning something really nasty, something vindictive. He wouldn't settle for anything less.

Surely Mom wouldn't let him do anything really wicked.

She was balking, but Floyd was winning.

It would solve a lot of problems.

Him, Marc. He was the problem.

How did Floyd expect to solve the problem of Marc? He'd suggested that his daughters might not be safe around him. The idea was embarrassing and infuriating. Marc didn't care anything about Barbara and Annette. He was no threat to them—but what if Floyd convinced Mom that he was?

Mom's words rang in his head: *I don't think I'm ready to do anything so drastic.*

"Drastic." That was a strong word. What had she meant by it?

Floyd hadn't argued against his plan, whatever it was, being drastic. What would *he* consider to be drastic? That meant extreme, didn't it? Marc knew with an icy certainty that Floyd wouldn't hesitate for a moment to do something extreme.

He tried to figure out what it could be. Locking him in his room and keeping him on bread and water? But Floyd couldn't expect to get away with anything like that. If Marc didn't go to school, eventually somebody in authority would come around and check.

What else would qualify as extreme?

Do you think I don't have any compassion for a child who's become troubled and unstable?

Compassion, no, it wasn't compassion Marc had detected in Floyd's nasty little smile. As for the reference to himself as "troubled and unstable," those words were menacing too. "Troubled"—yes, he'd admit to being troubled. There was no law against that, was there? Almost everybody was troubled, one time or another.

"Unstable" had a meaner connotation. People who were unstable were mentally off-balance. They gave them antipsychotic drugs. Sometimes they locked them away in mental institutions.

Mom would never agree to that. Never. But it would certainly be drastic.

Dad. He had to get ahold of Dad, tell him what was going on.

It was after eleven o'clock at night. Dad reported for work at seven in the morning, so he went to bed early. Still, this was important enough to disturb him, wasn't it?

Marc opened his bedroom door and listened. There were no lights, no sounds. His mother had gone to bed, but was she asleep? She'd said she couldn't sleep because she was so upset.

The hallway was carpeted, and his sock feet made no sounds as he made his way downstairs in the dark. The phone was in the living room, beside the chair where his mother sat to read or do embroidery. He had to have a light on in there, and since he didn't think his mother would notice it from her room, he turned it on so he could see to dial.

He'd memorized his dad's number and didn't have to look it up. He hadn't realized how heavily he'd counted on Dad's being his salvation until he listened to the phone ring, over and over, in an apparently empty house.

No óne was home? He'd expected them to be asleep, but to wake up when the phone rang. Where would Dad be at this time of night? And where was Grandma Belle? She went to bed earlier than Dad did, but she wasn't so deaf she wouldn't be awakened by a ringing phone.

He finally had to give up. Nobody was going to answer—not even a machine. How pathetic he was, that he'd have been relieved even to have been greeted by an answering machine!

He made his way back upstairs, and for the second time in a week he didn't bother to get undressed but just threw himself on the bed, and stared up into the darkness. Floyd's words continued to taunt him. Inexplicable, scary.

You can trust me to take care of this so that we can go on with our lives together.

Without the nuisance of dealing with Marc, he meant. But how did the man plan to get Marc out of their lives entirely?

Not even Floyd would contemplate murder.

But what else would permanently eliminate him from what was left of his family?

He heard his mother get up and cross the hall to the

bathroom, then return and softly close her bedroom door.

She wasn't sleeping. He wasn't sleeping. Marc squeezed his eyes tightly shut against the hot, stinging tears.

Please, Mom! Please don't trust him, don't listen to him, don't let him do whatever horrible thing he's planning.

Never in his wildest imagination could he have conjured up the truth.

11

Marc knew that Floyd continued to pressure his mother to agree to whatever his plan was to get her son out of the house.

They always stopped speaking when he entered a room. His mother showed the stress of lack of sleep, of worry. Marc wanted to blurt out the question, bring it into the open, demand to know what they were setting up, but he didn't quite dare do it. Maybe, if he kept a low profile, they'd forget it, whatever it was.

Yet deep inside, the insidious conviction grew that Floyd was winning.

Once he heard the man ask, "Do you want to talk to them yourself, Patricia? I can set that up."

Them? Who? Marc waited, breath held painfully, for her response.

"No, I don't want to talk to them."

"They'll reassure you. Nothing bad will happen to him. He'll be perfectly safe."

Why did that statement convince Marc that whatever Floyd's scheme was, just the opposite would happen? *He would not be safe.*

How would he not be safe? Physically? Mentally? What could Floyd do that would be legal?

Marc was going mad thinking about it, trying to sleep

without having nightmares, unable to concentrate on anything at school. Who cared about French verbs or learning math without a calculator? Who cared who won the baseball game or if he remembered to come in when it was his turn on a chorus?

He couldn't produce any correct answers when he was called upon; he wasn't even aware of what the question was.

He confided in Toby, who was shocked to his roots. "They couldn't do anything very bad," he insisted. "They wouldn't do anything that would get them in trouble with the law."

Marc hoped not, but he couldn't shake the dread.

He tried again, in the daytime, to call his father at work. The voice that answered was not Hank Solie's. "Uh—this is Hank's son. Could I speak to him? It's an emergency."

"Sorry," the clipped tones came over the wires. "Hank's taking a few days off. You can try him at home. You have that number, right? I can't give it to you."

"Nobody answers at home," Marc said, not even trying to conceal his disappointment. "Can you give him a message, then?"

"If he checks in, I'll let him know you called," the voice said, and cut the connection.

Dad wasn't at work and wasn't at Grandma's house. Where could he possibly be?

He considered talking to Pastor Collins, but it had been so long since he'd been to church he was ashamed to ask for help there. Besides, if he thought there was any merit to Marc's concern, Pastor's first move would undoubtedly be to speak to his mother. Who was being brainwashed, day by day.

Marc felt her losing. She was hardly eating; full, balanced meals slid off the agenda. She didn't bake anything, and had gone back to opening a can of soup and toasting a sandwich.

He remembered with longing, the days when he'd been able to talk to her about anything. Now it was as if his throat were paralyzed, unable to produce words of any significance.

And then it finally all came to a head, in the middle of the night.

He was sound asleep, and the overhead light came on, and Floyd stood there looking down on him.

"What—" Marc rolled over, holding a hand over his eyes.

Floyd was smiling tightly. "Come on, fella, get up. Get dressed."

He turned his head to look at the clock. It was ten minutes to two. "It's the middle of the night!"

"We've got a long ride," Floyd said. "Don't waste my time. Get up."

He was groggy, disoriented. For a moment he considered the possibility that this was another of the nightmares—Floyd had featured prominently in them—but then Floyd's hand came down hard on his shoulder, pulling him into a sitting position.

Suddenly fully awake, Marc realized it was not a dream. It was real. Floyd was here in his bedroom at two o'clock in the morning. Then something else registered: Across the hall, he heard his mother weeping.

"Mom? Mom, what's going on?"

"Don't bother calling your mother. Put your clothes on. You're going with me."

Marc raised his voice, unable to conceal his panic. "Mom! Mom, what's happening?"

Marc had laid out his school clothes, the way he always did. Floyd flung them at him. "Hurry up. Put them on."

For a guy who looked like such a wimp, Floyd had strong, steely fingers. He was, after all, a mature man with a man's muscles, which were more powerful than his own.

He had slept in his shorts and a T-shirt. He accepted the jeans and put them on, then his socks, and finally the plaid shirt, crumpled beside him on the bed. "What—what do you want? Where are we going?"

"To a place where you won't be able to cause any more problems, because the people there know how to deal with kids like you," Floyd said. "Your suitcase is already in the car. Your mother packed it yesterday. They said not to bring much, just jeans and underwear. Put your shoes on."

Mom had packed him a suitcase? Yesterday? Was that why she'd been so depressed at supper time? Why she'd scarcely spoken to him? She'd known Floyd was going to do this?

Numbed, unresisting, Marc allowed himself to be herded down the stairs. He called out to his mother as he passed her open bedroom door, but she didn't respond except with a fresh outburst of sobs.

"Mom, don't let him do this! Mother!"

The blue Caddie was parked in the driveway. Floyd opened the passenger-side door and shoved him inside, then walked around to the other side and got in. Marc heard the click as he locked all the doors.

"Where are you taking me?" he demanded, fully awake now, fully aware of the implications. "My dad'll find out and rescue me."

"Fine," Floyd said, shifting into reverse to back out onto the street. There were no lights in the houses around them. No witnesses. Not even a dog barked. They were all used to Floyd and his car.

Marc twisted around and looked back. Now that they had left the house, there was a light on in the upstairs bathroom, where his mother was maybe finally taking a sleeping pill so she could get some rest.

How could she? How could she have not only allowed Floyd to kidnap him, but have helped him by packing his bag ahead of time?

He hoped her guilt would keep her sobbing until dawn. He hoped she never slept again. And the fear that had been growing in him all week—for longer than that, actually—was a deep, cold shadow all through him.

"Fasten your seat belt," Floyd commanded as they headed out toward Highway 101, which swept through the town, going north.

"Why?" Marc asked bitterly. "If we have an accident and I get killed, it'll solve your problems, won't it?"

"Fasten it," Floyd said. And after a moment, Marc did.

They went north as far as Arcata, then took 299 to the east. The signs lighted under their headlights: REDDING 154 MILES. Practically the only other traffic was eighteen-wheelers. Once Marc spotted a white and blue he thought was a K & M—for all the good it did him.

He willed himself to calm down, to think, but it was all a jumble, and the fear grew and grew until he was so sick to his stomach he had to keep swallowing to keep from throwing up.

Highway 299 was a twisting, curving road through the mountains. He was glad he'd fastened the seat belt because he kept being thrown from side to side. Floyd drove fast—sometimes over the posted limits on sharp corners—and volunteered no information at all.

They went through Willow Creek and Burnt Ranch and Weaverville and Whiskeytown. Marc began to feel the need to empty his bladder, but Floyd showed no sign of stopping. He wished he'd thought to grab a jacket, for though it was late May the night air in the mountains was cool. He was used to very moderate temperatures on the coast, and didn't always bother with a jacket, but that was when he was moving, running, or riding a bike. His misery grew by leaps and bounds.

The thought came to him that Floyd was taking him somewhere into the wilderness to kill him.

He realized at once that this couldn't possibly be so. His mother would never have stood for anything violent. Floyd wouldn't do anything that would get him arrested.

They wouldn't have packed a suitcase if he weren't going to need the clothes.

But the idea was so grim and so horrible that he couldn't quite suppress it either.

He finally couldn't wait any longer or he was going to ruin the blue plush upholstery. "I have to go," he said, mortified to hear his voice cracking.

Floyd immediately swung onto the shoulder, headlights showing tall black trees on either side of the road. "Don't step off the pavement. I think there's an embankment along here if you go over the guardrail."

The lock clicked, freeing him to open the door when they stopped. He got out and moved toward the back of the car, relieving himself over the metal railing. He'd had to go so bad he continued to ache even after he'd finished.

He could have run, he supposed. Except that there was nowhere to run to. He got back in the car and the locks clicked again, keeping him imprisoned.

It was a long ride before he saw the signs for Redding; dawn had begun to streak the eastern sky. What was there in Redding that they could be going to?

But they didn't stop in the town. Floyd swung the big car onto the interstate, I-5, and continued north at seventy miles an hour. There was considerably more traffic now, not all of it trucks. People going to work early. A few tourists in their RVs, beating the heat that would inevitably wash over central California once the sun was fully up.

It was light enough to see Floyd's face when the man

glanced toward him and finally spoke. "Aren't you curious about where we're going?"

Not trusting his voice, Marc remained silent.

Floyd made a sudden movement to open the caddy on the seat between them, flicking out a sheaf of papers. "Read about it," he suggested as they fell beside Marc.

He didn't want to, but he couldn't help it. He saw at once that they were printouts from a computer, the top pages in full color. "Educational Consultations: help for parents and professionals in the treatment of at-risk teens. Page 1 of 8."

At-risk teens? Was that what they considered him to be? Well, if he was at risk, whose fault was that? Mom's, certainly, and even Dad's, really, because he'd moved off and left him. And Floyd certainly hadn't helped.

It was light enough to read now. What he read was appalling.

"We specialize in re-directing children making poor decisions—focus on emotional growth and character building in programs specifically designed for teens who have resisted other forms of treatment. Includes long and short term residential and wilderness programs, highly structured therapy boarding schools, psychiatric facilities for children with behavior and emotional problems. Emphasis is on teaching of self-discipline, consequences, responsibility, accountability, and improved self-esteem—"

Marc's vision glazed, and he blinked until he could see clearly again.

He knew what the words meant, but he couldn't relate them to himself. What poor decisions had he made? To have his sister die? His mother practically lose her mind in grief over it? To have his parents disagree over the preservation of Mallory's room as a shrine, to refuse counseling, and decide to divorce? How had he had any control over any of that?

Crashing into Floyd's car had been an accident, not a conscious decision to cause damage. Taking the jackknife to school had been a stupid oversight. His schoolwork had gone downhill because he was upset and couldn't think straight. He didn't fit into any of the categories mentioned: "ADD, ADHD, learning disabilities, emotional abuse"—well, maybe his parents had been guilty of *that*—"hyperactivity, in need of behavior modification, troubled teens. We offer residential treatment center or wilderness camps. Information about places that work with these children is available on this Web site."

There were books advertised dealing with the subjects mentioned that could be ordered on-line.

The cramp in Marc's chest was growing, and taking deep breaths didn't help.

He dropped those first pages and came to another set of computer printouts. This set was from a different Web site, with the picture of a man in camouflage clothes, smiling into the camera, projecting power and strength.

"Captain Jonas Jasper, commander," said the caption. And the heading across the top of the page was "Camp Heritage." Smaller letters read "Guidance and discipline for troubled youth. Character building. Strengthening of mind and body. Our staff specializes in disturbed boys and their problems. Fifteen years' experience in bringing these children through their crises and returning them acceptably to society. Located in the beautiful Trinity Mountains in Northern California."

There was more, pages of it, but Marc could no longer focus on the printouts.

He'd heard about "wilderness camps." They were military-style prison camps, some of them as brutal as boot camps, with "instructors" used to disciplining men who had refused to knuckle under to Army commands until forced to. Force. That was the primary thing that stuck in his mind. They relied on force.

He was being sentenced to this imprisonment without benefit of trial. The only juror or judge was Floyd, whom he wouldn't trust to care for a sick cat.

Mom, how could you trust him? How could you think I deserved anything like this?

They drove on into the morning as the temperature rose and Floyd turned on the air-conditioning. It was almost too cold, but Marc didn't protest. He was even colder inside, his very soul packed in ice.

He should have tried harder to reach his dad. He should have talked to Pastor Collins, or Miss Merritt, the counselor at school. To anybody—Toby's folks or his old Sunday school teacher, Mr. Everett.

He cleared his throat. "When I don't show up for school, they'll investigate."

"Yes," Floyd said with satisfaction. "We've already told them where you're going. They'll have teachers at

Camp Heritage so you won't get behind in your classes."

"And what'll you tell my dad?"

"When he asks—if he asks—we'll think of something," Floyd assured him.

If he asks. The tears rose again, hot and stinging. *Dad, where are you? Why have you forgotten me? Please, please! Come and find me!*

12

When he'd driven up this highway before, with his father, they had admired the scenery. It was spectacular when they passed through the Lake Shasta area. Shasta was a man-made lake, a reservoir, really, storing precious water behind a dam for the use of Southern California.

It looked the same today: a brilliant turquoise, reflecting the hot blue of the sky, a jewel set in the red earth. Marc could look down on the pleasure boats— graceful sailboats, zippy little motorboats, houseboats— and watch the unconcerned vacationers enjoying their holidays.

"Maybe one of these days," Dad had said, smiling, "we'll come up here and rent one of those houseboats for a week—what do you think?"

"Yeah," Marc had enthused, "let's do it!"

There was no enthusiasm today, only dread.

If Floyd noticed the scenery, he didn't mention it. Floyd, no doubt, was concentrating on getting rid of him.

For how long? What had he agreed on, with this Captain Jasper at Camp Heritage? His mother must have signed the papers, because Floyd had no legal authority over him. Had they specified how many weeks, or months? Would they let him off early for good behavior, and how would he manage that, since he hadn't really done anything criminal to be incarcerated here in the first place?

The dirt road off I-5 was unmarked. Floyd slowed, taking it, and every muscle in Marc's body cramped. They must be almost there.

Now they crept along, protecting the Cadillac from sharp bumps, winding downward through thick stands of pine and cedar. Finally they came to a gate, which stood open. There was a rustic sign overhead that said CAMP HERITAGE.

At first he could see nothing that looked like a camp. And then it became visible between the trees: several large log buildings and a couple of smaller ones. There was a camouflage-painted Humvee and a green pickup truck parked in front of one of the smaller structures, and a man in camos doing something near the truck. He turned and lifted an arm in greeting, and once more a wave of nausea swept over Marc. He hoped he wouldn't further disgrace himself in front of strangers.

Floyd eased the car to a stop and got out.

"Good morning," the man said. It wasn't the one who'd been in the picture on the computer printout, but a tall, well-muscled fellow with sandy hair and blue eyes that might have been faded by the sun. Marc guessed his age at about forty. He was wearing a baseball cap, only it was in a camo pattern that didn't match the rest of his outfit. "This would be Marc Solie arriving?"

"That's right," Floyd said. His voice was rich with fulfillment. "Might as well get out, Marc."

He wasn't sure his legs would obey his command to

move. But there was nothing to be gained by staying in the car. They'd only haul him out bodily.

"I'm Oberlin," the man said. "Hi, Marc."

He couldn't summon enough voice to respond.

"Just a minute, I'll get someone to see you settled in, then your father can come into the office and go over the rest of the paperwork."

"He's not my father," Marc said, unwilling to let that assumption stand.

"I'm about to become his stepfather," Floyd said smoothly.

"Oh. Good." Oberlin turned toward a boy, smaller than Marc, who was rounding the end of one of the larger buildings, carrying a plastic basket. "Britten, get rid of your laundry and come over here, please."

The boy obediently set the basket on the porch of the large building and trotted over. He was slightly built, maybe twelve years old, with brown hair that flopped forward over his face. "Yes, sir?" he said.

"This is Marc Solie. Find him a bed, see if he needs lunch, kind of clue him in, okay?"

"Yes, sir."

"This is Britten." Oberlin introduced them, and left Marc standing there with him while he and Floyd headed for one of the smaller buildings.

Britten stared him in the face. "Bummer, huh?"

"Yeah," Marc agreed. "You one of the inmates?"

"They call us cadets," Britten said. "Have you got a suitcase?"

"I guess it's locked in the trunk."

"We'll get it later. Come on," the younger boy said, and Marc went with him. Britten picked up his laundry and carried it into a large room furnished with chairs and tables and a couple of bookcases. Across that room they entered another lined on both sides with narrow beds covered in gray wool blankets.

"This is the barracks," Britten explained unnecessarily. "The bed next to mine's empty. You can take that." He rested the laundry basket on his own cot and indicated the next one over. "You get half the chest between our beds. Are you hungry?"

"I'm completely hollow, but if I swallow anything I'll puke," Marc told him.

Britten nodded. "Yeah. I felt the same way when I got here."

"How long have you been here?"

"Five and a half weeks."

"And is it considered impolite to ask what your crime was, that got you sent here?"

"No. Everybody knows why everyone else is here," Britten said. "My little brother was killed in a drive-by shooting, and I went ballistic. Smashed up some things. Couldn't seem to get it under control. They finally decided this place would calm me down."

"Has it?" Marc watched the other boy's eyes, somewhat reassured by the fact that though Britten was smaller and younger, he'd survived for five and a half weeks.

Britten shrugged. "I'm still pretty mad. I guess I still want to kill the ones who shot Billy."

"Do you know who they are?"

"I can't prove it, but I've got a pretty good idea."

"Do you have to get over wanting to kill somebody before they'll let you out of here?"

Britten considered. "I don't have to tell them what I'm thinking."

"What do they expect us to do?"

"Follow the rules. Don't make waves. We have anger management classes."

"Do they help?"

"No," Britten said. "But you learn what they want you to say when they ask questions."

"Psychiatrists?"

"No, I don't think so. They're supposed to be trained as counselors. One of them, Stoner, is just a thug, I think."

Marc's muscles tightened anew.

"Mean?"

"Yeah. I'd say so. If he tells you to do anything, jump however high he says. Don't sass him back. It's not worth it."

"The brochure said something about 'consequences,'" Marc said, remembering.

"Right. It's not worth the consequences." Britten sat down on his bed and began to more or less fold his laundry, placing it in the wooden chest between their beds. "Hope you don't mind if I put this stuff away. I want to do it before free time this afternoon. We're supposed to play baseball when the team finishes working on the swimming hole."

"There's a swimming hole?"

"Not yet, but we're building one. On the creek. We're damming it up, and it'll make a decent place to swim when it's finished. You play baseball?"

"At school," Marc said.

"I don't suppose you pitch?"

"No. Usually play one of the bases."

"Umm. Hoped you'd pitch. We don't have a good pitcher. McCloud always insists on pitching, but he's lousy."

"Why do you let him pitch, then?"

Britten grimaced, wadding his socks and stuffing them into the chest, unmatched. "He's nastier than anyone else. Not necessarily bigger, though he's a lot bigger than I am, but he's tough."

"What's he in here for?"

"Beating his old man to a pulp. Landed him in the hospital. Lost the sight in one eye."

"You mean McCloud, or his father?"

"His father lost the eye. He'll pick up anything that's handy in a fight. Guess he used a poker on his dad."

Marc sank uneasily onto his designated bed. "Do they have a lot of fights in here?"

"A few."

"Is there someone around to break them up when one starts?" He'd done his share of wrestling and horsing around, in fun, but he was no fighter.

"They don't usually break them up unless they get really bloody. Klammer says they hope we'll kill each other and they won't have to bother with us. But as much as they charge to keep us here, you'd think they'd want to keep us alive so the money would keep coming in. You want to play ball when the gang gets back?"

Marc hesitated. "I'm pretty wired. I didn't know Floyd was going to bring me here until two o'clock this morning. I don't know if I'd play very well."

"Most of us don't," Britten said. "But you're new meat. They'll be glad to have another player. We don't have enough guys for two full teams."

Marc didn't commit himself. He wanted to get a glimpse of the rest of the inmates. "Are we all in this one dormitory?"

"Barracks. This is the barracks. Yes, this is all of us."

Marc swiveled around to count beds. "Twenty of us?"

"Eighteen, now that you're here."

"That's enough for two teams."

"Privett won't play. Hates physical games. Furious because he can't have his computer here, his games and his e-mail."

"What's he in for?"

"His dad remarried and he's got stepsisters. He won't leave them alone, so they put him here."

"Rape?" Marc asked hesitantly, horrified.

"No, no, nothing like that. Keeps cutting up their clothes, tying their stockings in knots, cutting the buckles off their shoes, pours bleach in their shampoo bottles. Stuff like that. There's another empty bed next to Privett, but I thought you might like me better."

"Thanks." Outside, an engine started up, and Marc stood. "If that's Floyd leaving, I better get my suitcase."

It was. Marc stood on the steps and stared at the man who had delivered him here. "My luggage," he suggested.

Floyd stuck his head out the open window. "Oh, yeah. Might as well leave it all here," he said, and got out and opened the trunk.

By the time Marc had unloaded his belongings into the chest, there were voices of boys returning from the swimming pool project. They trooped in, stopping in a cluster around Marc and Britten.

"This is Solie," Britten said. "You'll get to know the others. Everybody has to wear a name tag all the time, except in the shower or when you're in bed."

He saw their name tags: big letters, blue on white, encased in plastic. Last names only.

Privett stared at him insolently. He was a scrawny redheaded kid with lots of freckles. "What you in for?" he demanded.

Marc was tempted to tell him it was none of his business, but Britten had said everybody knew all the dirt about everybody else, so he figured he might as well get it over with. "My mom's thinking about getting married again to a guy who hates my guts. He talked her into this."

"But what did you *do*?" Privett persisted.

"Talked back. Scraped the paint off the door of his precious Cadillac. Took a jackknife to school so they called the cops." It didn't sound like much compared to beating your father with a poker and putting his eye out. Or destroying your sister's belongings.

Privett's mouth twisted in scorn. "A cream puff," he pronounced, and stalked off.

"I'm supposed to apologize for being here under false pretenses?" Marc asked. "For not having killed somebody?"

A taller, thicker boy with dark hair spoke up. His name tag read CHERON. "He's a head case. Don't pay any attention to him. Nobody else does."

"Does he still do stuff like that here?" Marc wondered aloud. "Like he did at home?"

"Tie people's clothes in knots? Better not touch any of mine or I'll beat the crap out of him," Cheron said, and moved on to a bed down the line.

"Come on," Britten said, "let's play ball."

"Can you pitch?" the one called Klammer asked.

"No," Marc said, at the same time as the dark, chunky one—McCloud?—said, "Hey, *I'm* the pitcher."

"Not if we say you're not," Klammer informed him. He was sharp-featured, sturdy. "And we got enough to split into two teams. I'll take Solie on mine, and I'll pitch against you myself if you want your own team."

Behind him a couple of the other boys groaned, but nobody argued.

Marc decided he'd play, after all. If they had baseball, and were constructing a swimming hole, and he didn't cross anybody, maybe he had a chance of making it, for however long it lasted.

13

Marc had never been a star on the school team, but he'd been adequate. In this group, he was practically a pro. His first time at bat he struck out, but the second time around he hit a home run.

They screamed in delight. At least his team did. Their opponents were sore losers. But by the time they broke for supper, everybody seemed to have gotten over it.

Back at the barracks, Britten said, "We're expected to wash up, at least, before we eat. Showers are mandatory in the morning; you can take another one at night if you want to."

They traipsed over to the other large building for their meals, sitting at several big round tables with plastic tops. Supper that first night was meat loaf, mashed potatoes, peas with little onions in them, and coleslaw. A couple of people threw rolls at each other, but for the most part everyone behaved.

The staff, six strong, sat at a matching table at the far end of the room. Marc sat between Britten and Privett, who paid no attention to him.

"They look like ex-Marines," Marc said, studying the camouflages at the far table.

"Well, I think Stoner was. Rumor has it he was dishonorably discharged, but I don't know if it's true or not. The one with white hair is Captain Jasper. He runs the place. That's Stoner just taking off his baseball cap. You met Oberlin when you came in. He teaches regular school subjects, and doubles as cook. We have to take turns as his helpers and for cleanup. The one with the bristly haircut and the thick glasses is Quincy—he teaches anger modification and usually supervises working on the swimming pool. The short guy is Phelps. He's ex-Army, like Jasper. He supervises whatever needs it, including calisthenics. Don't be fooled by his size. He can take on anybody. And the last guy, the bald one, is Montoya. He's kind of Stoner's stooge."

"And how do you keep from getting crossways of any of them?" Marc wanted to know. The food, to his relief, was pretty good, and his stomach was finally settling down so he could eat.

"Not everybody worries about it. I keep my mouth shut, don't draw attention to myself, and stay out of trouble."

It sounded like a good policy. Most of the boys talked freely among themselves, somewhat less than respectfully, but low enough so their voices didn't carry beyond their own tables. Their talk was liberally sprinkled with profanity—nothing Marc hadn't heard before, nothing he intended to emulate.

Because he was used to a shower before he went to bed, he opted for one now, though the sweat worked up during the ball game had dried and he didn't think he smelled too bad. Some of the guys just sat around the lounge area in the barracks, talking or playing one of the battered board games. Nobody was reading any of the used books available.

The shower, at the back end of the barracks, was a single open room with toilets along one side. There was no privacy whatsoever, as Britten pointed out.

They undressed in the sleeping area and walked naked to the shower. Marc was used to showers after PE, but not in a place as open as this; he felt self-conscious, though the others who were showering paid no attention to him or Britten.

He was glad he'd joined the younger boy, because the shower made him feel better. He'd have liked hotter water, though. After adjusting it the best he could, he asked, "Is this as warm as it gets?"

"Right. Never hot enough to scald anybody. Can't be used as a weapon," Britten said, soaping madly.

A weapon. That brought Marc back to reality. At least the zero-tolerance policy at school had kept him from having to worry about that.

Just as he rinsed his hair and prepared to step free of the mantle of water, Marc realized that a tall boy he remembered as Coleman had stepped into the adjoining area and turned on the water.

Coleman was the only black in the group, and appeared to be the oldest, maybe seventeen or eighteen. As he stood there, stark naked, Marc forgot to finish his shower.

Coleman was a rich deep brown, with short, tightly

curled hair, and he had the most striking male body Marc had ever seen. Not the overly sculptured stature of a bodybuilder, but with smooth and perfectly proportioned muscles beneath his dark skin.

Coleman turned, soaping his armpits, and saw Marc staring. "What are you looking at?" he demanded, clearly hostile.

Marc could hardly say he thought the guy was beautiful. He swallowed and reached up to turn off the water. "Nothing. Sorry, I was spacing out, I guess."

"Well, space out at somebody else," Coleman said, and turned his back.

Not until they were standing between their beds, putting on clean clothes, did Marc ask. "What's he in here for? Coleman?"

"Assault," Britten said.

"I hope he didn't take offense because I looked at him."

"Well, he hasn't assaulted anyone since he got here," Britten offered, "though when Klammer shot off his mouth once, Coleman knocked him into the wall." He considered that and added, "I don't think that was assault. He was provoked."

Marc determined not to provoke anybody, if he could help it.

There were some sensitive souls, though. A lot of them were touchy in the extreme. They didn't want anybody invading their space, which was not easy, considering how close together they all were. There was a lot of squabbling as everyone prepared for bed, some of it good-natured, some of it antagonistic.

"Hey, Coleman. Heard you and Phelps got into it. He have you doing extra push-ups?"

"No," Coleman said, turning back the covers on his bed, only two feet away from Marc. "He made a mistake about who threw that rock. I explained to him how he was in error."

"Oh. Well, you must have talked real sweet to him," the boy suggested.

"No point in our messing it up when he was wrong." Coleman turned then and looked directly at Marc. "You curious, Solie? You ask why I'm in here?"

Marc swallowed, wondering how to avoid any semblance of offense. "Uh, Britten said for assault."

"That's right. I got my girl pregnant, and her old man came after me with a tire iron. I'm not letting anybody pound my brains out with a tire iron, so I took it away from him, and used it the way *he* intended to. He spent three days in the hospital and sicced the cops on me." He slid his feet into bed but didn't lie down. "My dad talked him into agreeing that if I came here, he wouldn't bring charges against me in court."

What am I doing here? Marc wondered. He didn't belong in a place where people assaulted one another and got their girlfriends pregnant and beat people's brains in.

"When I get out of here," Coleman said, punching his pillow before he leaned back on it, "me and Cecily are gonna get married. Her mama doesn't believe in abortion, so she's not gonna make her do that, but they think she's gonna give up that baby for adoption when it's born. No way am I gonna let that happen. That's my baby. I'll get a job and take care of both of them."

"I heard you was monkeying around with the Humvee," Klammer said, pausing on his way back from the shower, his hair sopping wet as if he hadn't bothered with a towel.

"Oberlin says I got some mechanical ability," Coleman said. "He's gonna let me work on the cars here, and maybe go to school for it when I get out. A mechanic can support a family. That's more than Cecily's old man can manage to do."

He rolled over with his back to Marc and pulled the blanket over his shoulders.

The lights blinked once, and then five minutes later went out altogether. A few of the boys continued to talk for a few minutes before quiet finally descended on the barracks.

The bed felt strange, the blanket was scratchy where it touched his chin, and he could hear people breathing around him.

Somewhere, off in the distance, a night creature howled. Marc went rigid. "What was that?" he whispered, turning to his left.

"Coyote," Britten said. "We hear them a lot."

Britten, at least, spoke decent English. Most of the rest of them didn't know anything about grammar at all. He wondered if any of them had been going to school before they came here or if they were all truants and dropouts.

Marc thought about his father. Surely he'd call soon,

when nobody answered his e-mails once his computer was fixed. What would they tell him? He'd never known his mother to lie about anything, but would she dare tell him what they'd done with Marc?

Maybe they'd just tell him Marc was away at camp, and he'd think it was Scouts or church camp, and not worry. For how long might the deception last, though?

He dreamed that his dad arrived in a K & M truck and took him away.

But in the morning, when a record played reveille at 5 A.M., he was still there.

"We have an hour of calisthenics every morning, then showers, before breakfast," the helpful Britten explained.

Marc had thought he was in fairly good shape, but an hour of jumping jacks and push-ups and a lot of other stuff left him desperate for a rest. He didn't completely humiliate himself, but it was a close call. The warm water felt good on muscles made so tender he wondered what he'd do about them tomorrow, and the day after that.

Phelps kept them moving, determined to wear them out, and Marc was relieved to see that he wasn't the only one who was puffing and ready to drop.

Breakfast was buckwheat pancakes, as many as they wanted. The orange juice was frozen, but tasted good. "Now what?" Marc asked, praying it wouldn't be something too strenuous before he'd had a chance to recuperate. He'd forgotten he didn't rely on prayer anymore, but it was too late; he'd already prayed.

"Solie," Phelps said when they stood up from the table, "you're to report to Oberlin in the schoolroom this morning."

"Yes, sir," Marc said. He had the feeling he ought to salute, but nobody else had, so he didn't. Phelps might think he was being smart-alecky and order a bunch of push-ups.

Oberlin looked up with a smile when Marc entered the schoolroom, which was in the other half of the dining hall. Already he could smell something cooking for lunch in the kitchen in between, maybe spaghetti sauce.

"Morning, Solie. I have your transcripts here, so let's look them over and see what we can do to carry on with your schoolwork."

Floyd had planned thoroughly. His transcripts. Marc felt a fresh wave of hatred toward the man his mother had become so enamored of.

"I can't go on with the French, but we could handle Spanish. Languages are very useful," Oberlin told him.

"I had a little Spanish last year," Marc admitted. Actually, he'd liked it better than French.

"Okay. We'll go with Spanish, start with a little review. So we've got math and history and language arts—you seem to have been doing well in that."

"I like reading," Marc said.

"Good. How did calisthenics go this morning?"

How was he supposed to answer that? He settled on, "I lived through it."

Oberlin laughed. Maybe he wouldn't be so tough to work with.

"We'll spend a couple of hours on lessons, then you can join Sergeant Stoner's crew chopping wood," the teacher told him.

Chopping wood. He'd never done that, but it didn't look too hard, Marc thought.

He changed his mind five minutes into the exercise, which took place out in the woods about a half-mile from camp. Klammer and half a dozen other guys whose names Marc didn't remember had already been working for some time when he arrived.

"You know how to handle an axe?" Sergeant Stoner asked. He was big, when you got close to him, and his muscles practically split his short sleeves.

"No, sir," Marc said truthfully.

"Well, we need lots of firewood here, so you'll learn. Here, split that chunk of wood."

Feeling awkward, Marc hefted the axe—it was heavier than he expected—and swung it at the block of wood.

The axe bounced off, cutting nothing except the ground. Behind him, somebody snickered, and he felt the heat climbing his face.

"You do it that way and you'll amputate your foot," Stoner said. "Here, watch this."

He swung his own axe and the wood split evenly into two pieces.

Marc stared at him, helpless, having no idea what Stoner had done differently.

Stoner grunted in exasperation. "Watch how I hold the handle. Watch how I swing it."

Marc had to take two whacks at the next block of

wood before it split and left him shaky but triumphant.

Klammer's voice, right alongside of him, said, "I don't know why we need to chop all this wood. I'll be long gone from this place before we need to burn any of it."

"Shut up and chop," Stoner said.

"We ain't allowed to talk today?" the boy asked arrogantly.

"Not unless you stay civil. Klammer, where's your water bottle?"

"I don't know. Guess I forgot it."

"You know the rules. Anytime you leave camp on a job, you carry a water bottle. You get dehydrated, it'll cost you a hundred push-ups. I suppose you forgot your hat, too."

"Yeah. Gettin' up so danged early in the morning, my brain don't work right."

"Never noticed that it worked too good anytime," one of the other boys said.

Marc tried to ignore their bickering. His arms were already tired and sore from the calisthenics, and it took all his concentration to split the wood, but at least Stoner wasn't hanging over him, criticizing every move. Sweat began to trickle down out of his hair and into his eyes.

They split the wood, and they stacked it on a cart to be hauled back to camp. It was a relief to switch from the first job to the second and give one set of muscles a rest. Lunch was eaten from brown bags they'd brought with them, sitting on the ground. Cheese sandwiches, apples. A small bag of chips. Marc drained his water bottle. "Are we allowed to go refill these?" he asked.

"You can refill it on break," Stoner said.

Marc looked directly at the man and saw something he'd missed earlier: Stoner was wearing a whip attached to his belt.

It was a wicked-looking thing, coiled up like a snake, long enough to reach maybe twenty feet or more.

When Stoner turned away to do something, Marc asked the boy next to him—the name tag said JOHNSON—"Does he ever use that whip on a kid?"

"Never saw him," Johnson said. "Not on a cadet. I saw him knock a blue jay out of a tree with it once, though. Killed it deader'n a wedge."

Marc glanced at the others for confirmation of this. "No kidding?"

"I seen him whip tin cans off a fence post with it," another boy said. "Klammer, he's stupid enough to keep pushing old Stoner till the guy uses it on him."

"He ain't allowed to use that kind of punishment," Klammer said with a snort.

"Me, I don't want to bet on that," Johnson said.

"He has to follow the rules too," Klammer said sourly. "You guys are just sissies."

Marc had never thought of himself as a sissy, but in this crowd he probably qualified. He and Britten and maybe Privett. The rest of them were thugs who belonged in jail instead of in a wilderness camp.

He wasn't sure about Coleman. Coleman was better-spoken than most of the others, and he exuded a sort of presence, a sense of composure, that Marc had to admire.

What would *he* have done if some guy had come at him with a tire iron, intent on beating him senseless?

He wasn't as strong or as well-coordinated as Coleman; he wouldn't stand much of a chance against a grown man. Yet he didn't think he could just stand there and let somebody batter him into a coma. If he could wrest the tire iron away from his opponent, he thought he'd give it his best shot.

Everybody had to be there for the anger management classes. They sat in a circle, on metal chairs, most of them slouched in an attitude of contempt for their instructor. Quincy was like the others: military bearing, looking as if he could do a hundred push-ups on one hand without raising a sweat, a bristly haircut, thick black-rimmed glasses that did nothing to detract from the tough look.

Marc thought Quincy might tell them to straighten up, but he didn't seem to notice how slovenly they appeared.

"Why don't we start with Mr. Klammer," Quincy said pleasantly enough. "Why don't you tell us why you're here, Mr. Klammer."

Klammer wore his cargo pants so low they were practically falling off. He scowled. "How come we have to start with me? I had to talk last time."

Quincy regarded him calmly. "I thought maybe you'd had a change of outlook since then."

Klammer swore. It went unrebuked. Apparently Quincy didn't worry about profanity. "What's to change, man? My old man got drunk and beat on me all the time from when I was a little snot-nosed kid, hadn't done anything except just *be*. So I finally got big enough to return the favor. I broke a chair over his head and the fight went out of him."

Quincy remained composed. "You broke his arm and gave him a fractured skull."

Klammer shrugged. "Yeah, well . . ."

"You do realize that we can't let you leave here until you learn to control your temper."

"Yeah. But you have to kick me out when I'm eighteen. Only three years to go." He grinned, seemingly with good humor.

They skipped around the circle. Quincy didn't lose his cool, no matter what any of the boys said. Marc didn't hear any regrets, genuine or otherwise. They all seemed to feel justified in having done whatever had landed them here.

There was a pattern to their stories: neglect, abuse, mostly by fathers, occasionally by mothers. Not one normal-sounding family in the bunch, as far as Marc could tell.

Remembering his own frustrations in far less threatening circumstances, he felt an uneasy shifting of his attitude—not toward Floyd and his mother, but toward these boys. Cheron looked as if he'd had his nose broken, and Marc speculated on how that might have happened. Cheron had had an abusive uncle who'd cornered him in his own bedroom.

"Once," Cheron said, "I told him if it ever happened again, I'd kill him."

"You see any way around that decision now?" Quincy asked.

A slow grin spread over Cheron's face. "I figured out a coupla ways to do it."

"I don't see much progress here, Mr. Cheron."

"Okay. You figure out how to put that pervert in jail for the rest of his life. That'll be progress," Cheron stated.

"Did you ever consider telling someone what was happening? Your parents? A teacher? Your grandmother?"

Cheron lost his smile. "You don't know my grandma," he said, and everybody laughed.

Marc didn't see how any of this was helping much. He didn't know if he'd have had the guts to try to solve his problems in the ways these other guys had, but he was beginning to understand why they'd done what they'd done.

He was glad when the first anger management session ended, solving nothing so far as he could see. He was glad Quincy hadn't called on *him*.

14

Some of Marc's fears diminished, though not all of them.

He was glad he had to report to Oberlin for school classes for a couple of hours after the 5 A.M. calisthenics. He felt lucky to get through that without collapsing. He was careful not to look at anyone in the shower. If anyone looked at him, he didn't want to notice. He got better with the axe.

He didn't join in the conversations, if you could call them that, with the wood-chopping crew. They were mostly acrimonious, everybody cutting everybody else. Stoner didn't seem to care about that as long as they kept swinging those axes.

Toward the end of the first week, there was an accident.

When the boy alongside Marc, Martinez, swung his axe, instead of the sharp crack of splitting wood there was a different sound, and Martinez screamed.

Marc looked over and saw blood spurting and the axe anchoring the boy's foot to the chunk of wood he'd been aiming at.

Stoner was there in seconds. "Well, Martinez, you been wanting out of Camp Heritage. I guess you just punched your ticket to a hospital." He glanced toward Marc. "Give me your T-shirt, Solie."

Marc whipped it off, heart pounding, feeling sick at the sight of all the blood.

Stoner quickly fashioned a thick pad of the shirt and slapped it on the wound. "Hold that here, hard," he told Johnson, who was the next man over.

Fortunately there was little wood stacked on the cart yet, and Stoner lifted a white-faced Martinez onto the end of it.

"Axes on the cart, everybody," Stoner said. "Everybody pushing or pulling. Back to camp until we can get another leader out here."

Marc joined the pushers, glad Stoner hadn't picked him out to hold the bloody rag that was his shirt. He thought Martinez was passing out, he lay so still. He was dark-skinned, but his outstretched hand, unmoving, looked as if it had already been drained of blood.

They made the hike back to camp, all of it uphill, mostly in silence. "Jeez," Johnson muttered beside Marc, "nobody'd deliberately put an axe through their foot just to get out of this place, would they?"

"Depends how bad you hate it here," Klammer said, putting his shoulder to the back of the cart.

"Not everybody's willing to stay for another three years," Privett said. "Some of us want to go home."

"You don't know what my home's like," Klammer snarled. "My old man's a drunk, my ma ran away two years ago, and my gramma peddles drugs. Who wants to go home?"

"I do," Privett asserted. "I've had enough of you

barbarians. No computers, no phones, no TV. This place is the pits."

Klammer snorted. "You wouldn't know the pits if they bit you. Just because nobody else is a pervert."

Marc tried to concentrate on pushing the cart. He wondered if Martinez would bleed to death. The axe that had gone into his foot was lying on the bed of the cart, right under Marc's nose, liberally smeared with blood.

Captain Jasper came out of the office when they rolled into the yard, and Oberlin, too. They stood looking down on poor Martinez. Marc's T-shirt was a red, sodden mess atop the boy's mangled foot.

"You want me to call an ambulance?" Oberlin asked.

"No. It happened on my watch. I'll take him in," Stoner said. "It'll be faster than the aid car. Johnson can come with me and keep pressure on it."

Johnson was looking rather green, his hands immersed in the gore. "Can I wash first?" he asked.

"Yeah. Solie, fetch us a stack of towels," Stoner ordered, and Marc was glad to comply.

As they transferred him to the Humvee, Martinez roused enough to ask, "Am I going to lose my foot?"

"No. You're not going to be permanently crippled. No sitting back on your can and going on disability for the rest of your life," Stoner said. If the sight of the blood bothered him, it didn't show. "Okay, Johnson, you sit there and elevate that leg, keep his foot in your lap. Hold a couple of towels on it, like this." He demonstrated.

"Yes, sir," Johnson said. He was almost as pallid as Martinez.

Where would they have to go to a hospital? Back to Redding? Or was there one in Yreka, farther north? Nobody said.

The Humvee took off, rather slowly, up the dirt road.

"Okay," Captain Jasper said. "Let's go back to work, boys. Get the hose and rinse off the cart, Klammer. The blood will draw flies."

By this time the bald Montoya had come out, and he took command of the crew. They lumbered downhill, to where splatters on the wood marked the spot of the accident, and the axes were handed out again. Privett got the bloody one, making a face as he accepted it from Montoya's large dark hand. There was virtually no chatter the rest of the day.

Martinez didn't come back when Stoner did. Nobody volunteered any information about him, and nobody asked.

Marc dug out another T-shirt, wondering if he'd be expected to wash the stains out of the one that went along with Martinez. But it was never returned to him.

Gradually he got over the worst of the sore muscles from the wood-chopping and the exercises. He thought he must have lost a little weight, because he had to use a different notch in his belt.

The morning he realized he was whistling under his breath as he split wood, he paused for a moment to consider how unlikely that would have been only a few days ago.

It was still early morning, and the sun was getting hotter, making him glad for his baseball cap and the red kerchief he had tucked in it to protect the back of his neck. His arms were browner, and no doubt his face was too.

The air smelled good, of pine and spruce and cedar and dry grass that had its own pleasant aroma. If he hadn't been under sentence, here—an indefinite sentence, as far as he knew—he might have enjoyed being out on this hillside.

Except for having to work in the same crew as Klammer.

Klammer was a pain in the butt. He constantly screwed up, deliberately. He left items behind, for which he was forced to return, delaying everyone else. He spilled things—his milk might be dumped over into Marc's plate at lunch, and at dinner it might be Britten's.

"Oops!" he'd say. "Sorry."

He wasn't sorry. Not about that or anything else, like "accidentally" dumping bleach into the washer with Coleman's clothes, claiming he'd thought it was the machine with his own underwear.

Coleman was furious. He'd had a sweatshirt that he really liked, and it was ruined. Oh, it was still wearable, still warm enough for chilly mornings, but there were light splotches on the dark blue background.

He grabbed a handful of Klammer's shirtfront and was about to thrust him against a wall when Stoner walked into the barracks. The staff didn't usually intrude on the boys there; they were left to settle their own differences in their own way, for the most part.

"I ought to kill him," Coleman said. He'd stopped

shoving but was still gripping the shirt, as Klammer grinned up at him, intentionally provocative.

"Okay by me," Stoner said casually. "I see the anger management classes are taking."

"He poured bleach on my clothes. Half a bottle. They'll all fall apart."

"He's a jerk," Stoner said as if in agreement. "I've wanted to belt him myself, but it's against the rules."

Coleman considered. "It's not against the rules for me to do it?"

"Some rules are hard to enforce. Of course, you have to remember that it'll get you out of Camp Heritage and into criminal court. Into a penitentiary. I'm not sure you can get classes in auto mechanics there."

Coleman's large black hand relaxed slightly, then gave Klammer a shove as he let go. "He's not worth it."

"My thought exactly. Solie, we've had a phone call about you."

Marc snapped to attention. "About me? From who? Sir," he added belatedly.

"Says he's your father. Says he never signed any papers to put you here."

The drumming in his chest was deafening. "He didn't. Sir."

"Says he can unsign anything anybody else signed."

"Yes, sir." Maybe there was a God after all. "Is he coming to get me out?"

"Said to give you a message. He can't get here immediately, but he'll see you probably the first of next week. Think you can stand it that much longer?"

Relief exploded through him, leaving him limp and weak. "Yes, sir."

"Good." Stoner looked at Coleman. "As you were, cadet."

Nobody remembered any parent ever offering to unsign an order to commit anyone to Camp Heritage. Nobody remembered a parent ever coming to bail a kid out.

"I knew you were a cream puff," Privett said, looking down his freckled nose.

"As if you wouldn't give your eyeteeth to have somebody come and get you," Cheron said.

"Except," Klammer added, "your parents don't want you back. They probably hope you stay here until you die of old age."

"When you do get out," McCloud said, "you'll more than likely be committed to an asylum for the criminally insane. It's nuts to cut up girls' underwear and stuff their hairbrushes down toilets and put drain cleaners in their bathwater."

Privett glared at them all, then stalked away.

"Wish I had a dad cared enough to come get me," Johnson said. "Or a ma, either one."

Marc couldn't think of anything to say. He was overwhelmed, that Dad had discovered where he was, and knew he didn't belong here. He could get through one more week. He was sure he could. In fact, it would be a cinch.

And then Klammer spoiled it, and Stoner, and everything good he'd been hoping for was even farther out of reach than it had ever been.

15

Naturally, the boys—or cadets, as the staff called them—talked about their leaders.

Captain Jasper didn't figure much in their attentions. He occupied himself primarily with administrative duties; nobody could imagine what that entailed, in a camp with fewer than twenty boys, except handling the money. Everybody knew Camp Heritage was expensive. Marc wondered if Floyd was picking up the tab. He couldn't see how his mother could do it.

Oberlin was regarded as a pretty good guy, for a teacher. He seemed fair, and genuinely concerned that each boy got an education.

"He says it'll be easier for me to get along on the outside if I know how to read," McCloud reported. "Says I'll have a better chance of getting a job. Be able to leave home sooner. Cripes, I been in school eight years so far and I never learned to read, so I don't know why he thinks I can do it now, but I'm game to try. You think I can learn to read?" he asked Marc earnestly.

"I don't see why not," Marc said. He couldn't imagine anybody not being able to read. Thinking about the way some of the kids talked, he wondered how many of the rest of them, with the exception of Britten and Privett, couldn't read. "When I'm home and can get to a library, I read four or five books a week."

Several of the other kids looked at him as if he were exaggerating, though he wasn't. Only Britten nodded. "Me too," he said.

"Yeah, well maybe Oberlin's not a bad kind of guy," McCloud said.

Phelps was not popular. He pushed everybody to the breaking point with his calisthenics program. He was big on demanding push-ups and laps on the makeshift track. It annoyed him when Oberlin gave new kids a break by requesting their help with the kitchen chores if he thought they were at their limit of physical reserves and needed a rest.

Quincy drew mixed reviews. Nobody liked the anger management sessions. Either they thought they didn't need them—anybody'd get mad at someone who abused or otherwise mistreated them, or who tried to pound them into a pulp, wouldn't they?—or they thought he didn't know what he was talking about. He admitted, when McCloud asked point blank, that he'd never been personally abused. "Except by the United States Marines," Quincy said with a grin that robbed the words of complaint.

So what made him qualified to talk to kids who had plenty of reasons to resent those who had pushed them to the breaking point?

"But that kind of behavior is not socially acceptable," Quincy pointed out reasonably.

"It's acceptable for someone to get drunk and beat up

on his wife and kids?" a boy named Spatten demanded.

"No. It's not. But there are better ways to handle it than bashing in his head and getting sent to juvie. What else could you have tried?"

Nobody responded.

"Come on, guys, you all know the alternatives to violence."

"Counseling," Britten offered.

"Right. And where do you go for that?"

"A teacher," McCloud said. "A minister. Only I don't know no ministers. We don't move in the same social circles."

Several people giggled.

"A cop," Cheron said. "Only he comes to your house and talks to your old man, who beats the crap out of you as soon as the cop's gone."

"You can always talk to your grandma," Johnson suggested, straight-faced, "unless you got a grandma like Klammer's, who sells dope."

There was another ripple of amusement.

"There's always somebody you can trust, if you look for them," Quincy said. "Most of you don't like it here very much. You could avoid coming back—or graduating to prison—if you look for alternatives to taking the law into your hands. That is never going to be your best way to go."

They shuffled their feet, coughed, snickered. Nobody took Quincy seriously, though privately Marc thought he had a point.

Montoya was the only one of the staff who was

married, though Marc figured he must not spend much time with his wife, considering he hardly left camp until late in the evening. He was quiet, but firm. He expected the crew working with him on the dam to put in their time on the project and not shirk their work. He didn't put up with any guff, though he didn't make a fuss when the boys squabbled among themselves. Some of them tried to shock him with their language and filthy stories about their exploits—mostly imaginary or grossly exaggerated—but Montoya maintained a stoic calm.

And then there was Stoner.

Nobody was ambiguous about Stoner. To a cadet, they hated him.

"He's a sadist," Coleman said, and there were nods of agreement, except from McCloud, who asked, "What's a sadist?"

"A mean, unfair creep," Coleman said, "who does things just to make somebody else feel bad. You see the way he rests his hand on the handle of that whip? Dying to use it on any one of us."

Once in a while Stoner would unleash the whip, and show off with it. Each of them who observed one of these demonstrations was easily able to imagine it cracking down over his own shoulders, striping his back. And more than one of them went on to picture himself using it on Stoner.

Nobody doubted that Stoner enjoyed hurting people. He didn't like animals, either.

It was Privett who found the puppies.

It was Sunday afternoon. They'd been up at 5 A.M. for

their usual exercises, then sat for half an hour after breakfast for a talk by Captain Jasper that was supposed to pass for a religious observance, and now they were free after the midday meal. Some of the guys were dinking around the almost completed pool—it wasn't yet really deep enough to swim in, but the water was refreshing on their feet, or their trunks, if they sat down in it—and others were playing a game of work-up. They were disgusted that since Martinez was gone, they couldn't get up two full teams. Privett had gone for a solitary walk.

Marc decided it was too hot for running bases, and the pool was still too shallow to bother with. He was lying on his bed, reading one of the ancient books he'd found in the lounge, when Privett came in, carrying a nondescript small dog, white with black and brown spots.

Surprisingly, Privett addressed Marc, probably because he was the only occupant of the barracks at the moment.

"Look what I found. Somebody dumped off three pups. Two of them are dead, but this one's still alive."

Marc sat up, putting his book aside. "Is he hurt?"

"I don't think so. They've probably been out along the road for a while, dumped over the embankment below the road. He's awful skinny. His ribs are sticking out."

It was the first time Marc had had a conversation with Privett that wasn't acrimonious. "I've got half a sandwich left. I wonder if he'd eat it."

He reached for it and broke off a small bit. The dog

licked eagerly at his fingers, and Marc broke off another piece. "How old do you think he is?"

"Three months? Four?" Privett sounded practically normal. "I used to have a dog once. I had to get rid of it when my dad got married again. His new wife is allergic to dogs."

"Tough," Marc said, meaning it. He'd never had a dog, but he'd always envied Toby, who had two golden retrievers.

"He could be thirsty, if he was out there for very long. You want to hold him while I get some water?" Privett said, dropping the pup into Marc's lap.

The dog squirmed in his hands, turning to lick at him. Marc felt a thrill of excitement run through him, liking the soft, warm little body. He continued to feed him, and when the sandwich was gone, the dog licked at his chin.

Privett returned with an aluminum pie tin they'd carried cookies in from the dining hall. He accidentally spilled a little of it on Marc's bed, but Marc didn't care.

"Boy! He's going to burst," he said, watching the small sides swell as the puppy drank. "You going to try to keep him?"

"Naw. They'd never let me take him home with me, if I ever get out of this place. I'm not gonna get attached to another dog," Privett said. "Not unless I'm sure I can keep it."

At that point several of the ballplayers walked in. They were all instantly mesmerized by the dog. "Looks like a rat," Coleman said. "I've seen lots of rats in the basement of our building. Where'd he come from?"

"Privett found him. There were three, and the others were dead. We think somebody threw them over the guardrail, maybe several days ago."

"I had a dog once," McCloud said, reaching out a finger to stroke the soft head. "He got run over by a truck. Ma wouldn't let me get another one."

Privett stood indecisively for a moment, then asked Marc, "You want to try to keep him? If they'll let you. You're getting out next week. You could take him home with you."

The puppy, no longer thirsty or dying of starvation, had fallen asleep on Marc's lap. "You mean it?" he asked. He looked around the circle of observers. "You think they might let me keep him?"

"Ask Oberlin. He's more likely than anybody else to let you," Coleman proposed unexpectedly. "He might, seeing you're leaving soon."

So he asked Oberlin, reminding him that he'd only have to keep the dog in the barracks for a few more days. Oberlin grinned a little. "Why not?" he said. "Just keep him out from under Sergeant Stoner's feet. He doesn't like dogs much. A German shepherd bit him in the face when he was a kid, and he never got over it."

Marc scrounged a short length of rope and fashioned a makeshift leash. He talked Oberlin into letting him borrow a water bowl and a pan for food, and brought the dog scraps from the kitchen. There was always stuff they normally scraped into the garbage can, and while it wasn't necessarily ideal puppy food, the dog ate it and didn't throw up any of it.

Several people referred to the dog as "the rat," and Marc decided that was a good enough name. It went with his looks. "You can sleep with me," he told Rat, and the dog's tail wagged enthusiastically.

Marc was unprepared for the events that followed. Stoner scowled when he saw the dog, but Marc quickly said, "Oberlin said I could keep him, since I'm going home next week. He gave me dishes for him and everything."

"Well, keep him out from under my feet," Stoner said coolly. Marc was glad he hadn't asked permission from *him*.

The rope he was using for a leash was old and frayed. He wasn't sure it was strong enough to hold if the pup lunged against it, but maybe it would be good enough until Dad showed up to get him. Then they'd get a regular collar and a leather leash.

Rat wasn't housebroken, of course, so Marc took him along on whatever activity he was engaged in. None of the leaders except for Stoner seemed to care, once they'd been informed that Oberlin had given permission.

Marc tethered his new pet to whatever tree or post was nearby, and made sure Rat had water available all the time. He fed him when he had food himself. Rat wasn't allowed in the dining room, but Oberlin didn't care if he lay at Marc's feet during school sessions.

The fatal morning started out as usual, with wood to be chopped and loaded onto the cart. Rat lay in the shade to one side of the cutting area, nose touching his pie-pan water dish.

"As usual" encompassed Klammer's customary rule-breaking. He had forgotten his hat, and was not allowed to return to camp by himself to retrieve it. He'd brought his water bottle because Stoner had expressly reminded him to when they trooped back as a group to get the hat. When after they were all on their way again it was discovered that he had also "forgotten" his sack lunch, muscles bunched along Stoner's jaw.

"If you think you're going back again," he said, "forget it. You can do without lunch."

Klammer shrugged as if it were of no consequence. A few minutes later he "accidentally" knocked over the water bottle McCloud had set on the edge of the cart. He stood looking at it dribble out onto the ground, making a wet spot of darkening red earth.

"Hey!" McCloud protested, reaching the bottle to close it after half its contents had run out. "Now what am I supposed to drink, you idiot?"

"Take Klammer's bottle," Stoner decreed.

McCloud puckered up in distaste. "I don't want to drink after all his crummy germs!"

"Pour his water into your own bottle, and this time close the top so it can't spill."

A short time later, as Marc chopped steadily (it was easier now, either because he was getting used to it or because he was relieved that he wouldn't have to do it much longer), angry words broke out behind him.

Privett had discarded the jacket he'd worn earlier and placed it, with his lunch sack, on a log a few feet beyond their work area. Marc jumped when Privett suddenly shrieked in his ear.

"You stupid jerk, you did that on purpose!"

Everybody stopped working and spun around to see Klammer grinning and shrugging. "No I didn't. It was an accident."

"I've had about enough of your stupid 'accidents,'". Privett howled, and actually raised his axe as if to swing it as a weapon.

Stoner closed the distance toward Privett and jerked the axe out of his hands.

"Knock it off!"

"He deliberately stomped right on my lunch! Look, he squashed everything in it, and he went right through the bag! Tore it all up!"

"You still can't chop his leg off," Stoner said. He advanced on Klammer. "We've all had enough of you. You've been asking for it ever since you got here. Today you're going to learn about consequences."

"Yeah?" Klammer asked. To Marc's astonishment, he was still smiling, and he remembered something Quincy had said: "Everybody craves attention, in one way or another. It's a normal human need. But some of you are thriving on negative attention instead of working toward positive reinforcement. Don't settle for doing something wrong to make people notice you. Do something right."

That was Klammer. Negative attention. Do something hateful to provoke a reaction from somebody, even Sergeant Stoner.

Marc couldn't understand the need, himself. Why do something that was going to make somebody like Stoner murder you?

Stoner's face was grim and set. He wiped a big hand over his mouth as if trying to adjust it, to control his anger. "It's a good thing I've been through the anger management lessons, or I'd be tempted to use that axe on you myself," he said.

Klammer smirked. "You'd lose your job. You'd probably go to jail."

"Maybe," Stoner said. "But you'd still be missing a big chunk of your leg."

The sneer faded. For the first time, the other boys saw Klammer uncertain. He licked his lips.

"Give me your axe," Stoner said, holding out his hand.

Klammer hesitated, reluctant to relinquish it, but did not resist when the tool was jerked away from him.

The other boys stood in a hushed silence. Marc was aware of his own breathing, the stirring of the tops of the pines in the breeze, the heat that brought out the sweat on his forehead and his back.

Stoner carefully laid the confiscated axe on the back of the cart without looking at it, his attention fixed on Klammer. "Get down on your knees," he said in a voice so soft Marc scarcely made out the words through the thunder of blood in his ears.

Klammer swallowed. He didn't move.

"On your knees," Stoner repeated, and this time he reinforced the order by placing one of those powerful hands on Klammer's shoulder, shoving him down.

Klammer went down fast, nearly falling on his face, quickly scrabbling to regain his balance. There was no defiance in him now.

Stoner reached into a back pocket of his camos, pulling out a plastic device Marc recognized from TV: handcuffs.

"Put your hands behind your back," Stoner ordered.

There was not a sound as he knelt behind Klammer and put the cuffs on him.

Every boy in the group was paralyzed, hardly daring to draw a breath. Marc could smell sweat—sharp, acrid. His own, or someone else's?

Stoner looked around, then directed his remarks to Marc. "Get me the rope off your dog."

Marc opened his mouth in automatic protest, then thought better of it. "Yes, sir," he said. He didn't think Rat would run away, but he didn't see where he had any choice except to risk it.

He crossed to where Rat was tied and fumbled with the frayed rope. Rat licked at his face and stood up, but when Marc told him "Stay," he miraculously didn't move from the spot by his water dish.

Marc handed the short length of rope to Stoner, who stared at it in disgust. "Where'd you get this piece of crap?" he asked.

"It-it was all I could find," Marc stammered.

Stoner was still kneeling. He used the fragile old length of rope to tie Klammer's feet together. Then he stood and picked up the empty water bottle McCloud had emptied into his own container and set it on the ground about four feet ahead of Klammer.

"Look at it. Remember that it's empty because of your own misbehavior. Think about how good a drink would taste. Think about your sins that got you in here," he said, and turned his back. "Get back to work, everybody. We don't have the cart full yet."

For a few seconds, nobody moved. Then McCloud hit a chunk of wood with a forceful swing, and the others gradually returned to work as well.

Klammer crouched on his knees, unable to do anything else. All the fight had gone out of him. He kept his face expressionless. Marc couldn't feel sorry for him—he'd brought it on himself, and actually Stoner had been relatively patient with him. Klammer had been asking for it for a long time.

There was no bantering, no teasing, no complaining now. They all worked in silence until the cart was filled with the winter wood supply. "Okay," Stoner said in his normal voice. "Turn in your axes."

They were placed on the cart. "Push or pull," Stoner said.

Marc glanced at Klammer, whose T-shirt was soaked with sweat. His kneeling position was uncomfortable, muscles being pulled out of normal range, and he was beginning to pale beneath his tan.

It was Privett who voiced what was on all their minds. "What about Klammer? Are we leaving him behind?"

"He's got a lot of thinking to do," Stoner said. "Come on, put some muscle into this."

Marc glanced back, and saw that Klammer was afraid. He didn't see anything he could do about it, and he certainly wasn't going to speak up on his behalf, but he didn't think this was quite ethical, or approved behavior on the part of a staff member.

Nobody said a word as they moved the cart up the trail, through the woods to camp. The trees quickly blocked out their view of Klammer.

The area where they'd been cutting wood was far enough from camp that Marc didn't think anyone would hear Klammer if he yelled. How long did Stoner expect to leave him there?

It was really hot, the hottest day since Marc had been there. The water in his bottle was warm enough to be unpalatable, but at least it was wet. He thought about the empty bottle placed just in front of Klammer. Privett's discarded lunch bag was also out of his reach.

It would be possible, maybe, for the boy to scrooch himself forward on his face in the dirt, but it would be difficult. There was no way he'd ever make it all the way back to camp by himself.

They left the cart to be unloaded later, to add to the growing wood supply behind the dining hall. They all still had their lunch sacks, but nobody felt like eating. And obviously Stoner didn't care whether they ate or not.

"Dismissed," he said, and headed toward the office.

Nobody saw him come out. Nobody knew what to do next.

"You think he'll go back and untie him?" McCloud wondered in a half-whisper.

"Who cares?" Privett said, but without conviction; it was clear that even he had been shaken by the morning's events.

In silence the cadets refilled their water bottles. Their appetites were gone, but they were all moderately dehydrated, and the cooler water was welcome.

A game of baseball was out of the question. When the crew came in from the dam building project and reported that they were all returning in their swimsuits, because they'd installed the final top layer of rocks to bring the pool up to the desired depth, nobody from the wood-chopping detail was interested. And even some of Montoya's crew became subdued when they heard the report about Klammer.

"Nobody likes him," Coleman stated without argument, "but I don't think they're supposed to stake us out like goats for the coyotes to get."

They kept an eye out, unobtrusively, for Stoner to go back. But he didn't. He sat talking to Oberlin, and then to Montoya. Finally he spent some time with Quincy.

There was a thermometer on the outside of the dining room, and the red line crept up and up. "One hundred and four," Marc read it off, "and that's in the shade."

Nobody voiced the thought, but they were all aware that Klammer was not in the shade.

By four o'clock, with the mercury still stuck at 104, Marc knew he had to go back.

16

When he stood up and took the first few steps toward the path leading back to the woodlot, everybody knew what was on his mind.

"You gonna go check on him?" Coleman asked in a hushed tone.

Marc swallowed, then paused for another drink. He'd been parched ever since they'd come in, and he kept thinking of Klammer, tied out there in the sun with an empty plastic water bottle.

"Yeah," he said, his voice cracking.

"If Stoner catches you, he may tie you out there too," Coleman pointed out.

"Yeah," Marc repeated.

For a matter of seconds they all stared at him, gathered there on the porch in front of the barracks door.

Privett was the only one who stood up. "You want me to go with you?"

The offer was so unexpected that Marc swallowed again, hard. He hadn't realized until he rose to his feet just how difficult this was going to be. Yet the compulsion was strong; he couldn't ignore it. Having company made it only marginally less terrifying, but he was grateful for Privett's offer.

"Sure," he managed, and the other boy fell into step with him.

Nobody was moving around the camp. In the heat all the instructors had vanished inside, though it was scarcely any cooler in any of the buildings: There was no air-conditioning, even in Captain Jasper's office.

The first part of the walk was through the trees, which offered intermittent shade but no relief from the heat. Usually there was a little air moving the tops of the pines and cedars, but at the moment it was as still as death.

Sweat soaked his clothes. Even his hair was wet when he ran a hand through it. It was criminal to have left Klammer out there in the sun, Marc thought desperately. Without even knowing he was doing it, he began to pray. *Please, don't let him be dead. Please.*

Pine needles muffled their footsteps. Red dust rose in small puffs when they got off the carpet of needles.

Halfway there, Privett cleared his throat. "It was my fault, wasn't it?"

"What?" Marc couldn't make the mental connection, so filled with dread was he.

"Stoner wouldn't have punished him that way if I hadn't been yelling about him stomping on my lunch bag."

"He spilled McCloud's water," Marc reminded him.

"But Stoner didn't punish him until I yelled about my lunch."

"He brought it on himself," Marc said, as if trying to convince himself that the punishment was appropriate.

He glanced at Privett and saw that the other boy was extremely pale. There were beads of moisture on his forehead. And suddenly he doubled over, retching, dry-heaving. There was nothing to come up except a little water.

Marc paused. Privett dropped to his knees, clutching his stomach, making a sobbing sound. Marc saw that Rat had followed them, trailing uncertainly behind.

"Go home," Marc said, as sternly as he could manage, but Rat stood his ground, tail wagging tentatively. If he took him back, shut him in the barracks, somebody on the staff might see him. Stop him. He decided to ignore the dog.

There was nothing he could do about Privett, either.

After a moment, Marc left him there, crying. He was too petrified to cry himself, too filled with anxiety, to offer words of reassurance. He couldn't let himself think what would happen if Stoner found him out here.

As he approached the clearing, he had to struggle to make the sounds, to call out.

"Klammer? You okay?"

There was no response.

A moment later he walked out from the trees and into the area where the fallen trunks awaited cutting into firewood.

Klammer was not where Stoner had left him. He had managed to worm his way perhaps twenty yards, knocking over the empty bottle Stoner had left to taunt him. He was sprawled facedown in the dirt, hands and feet still tied behind him.

Marc covered the distance between them in long, quick strides, dropping to his knees to reach out and touch the other boy.

He was warm to the touch. For a moment Marc's heart swelled with relief, and then he sought for a pulse, and could not find one.

He was warm, so he must be alive, Marc reflected. But then, he suddenly thought, under the broiling sun, why would a body cool off, even in death?

Marc's gorge rose, and he moved his fingers from Klammer's wrist to that point on his jaw where the cops in movies always found a pulse.

Nothing.

Panic swept through him. What would happen now? Klammer looked so helpless lying there with his face in the dirt. His arms were twisted behind his back. His ankles were still tied together with the flimsy rope.

A part of him told Marc he should remove the plastic handcuffs and the rope. Another, more rational part told him not to touch them. They were evidence. Evidence that Stoner, in his rage, had passed the boundaries of common sense and caused this boy to die.

A stick cracked under a heavy foot, and Marc spun around to see Stoner emerging on the path from camp.

Still crouching, Marc looked up, his heart trying to tear its way out of his chest.

"He's dead," Marc croaked. "You killed him."

"Get away from him," Stoner said. He jerked the water bottle off the strap that held it to his belt. "All he needs is a little water."

Marc stood up, shaking uncontrollably. "It's too late. He's dead. It must be a hundred and ten degrees out here, and you left him with no water. For hours and hours. He must have had heatstroke."

Something flickered in Stoner's face. Apprehension at last? Realization that Marc was right?

Stoner strode forward, and Rat, not understanding but sensing that something was wrong, tried to dart past him to reach Marc.

The dog got tangled in Stoner's large feet, making the man stumble. Rat yipped, and in his confusion got square in Stoner's way.

Frustrated—perhaps in a panic of his own?—Stoner kicked him, with all his strength.

Rat flew through the air and landed between the instructor and Marc, raising red dust when he landed and lay motionless.

Stoner continued to advance, viciously kicking Rat again as he passed, heading straight for Marc and the lifeless Klammer.

At that point instinct took over. Marc thought that both his dog and the obnoxious boy were dead, and that by the look on Stoner's face, he was going to be next.

He looked around wildly for any sort of weapon, but the axes had already been taken back to camp. He picked up a chunk of wood and threw it, but it bounced off Stoner's chest with no apparent effect.

Stoner didn't need a weapon to kill him. He could do it with his bare hands. As a trained soldier, his hands were lethal weapons.

And then Marc saw it. The branch had been tossed aside as fit only for kindling, not to be chopped into stove-size pieces, but it was fairly thick and sturdy, about four feet long.

He scrabbled backward and snatched it up, then swung it with all his strength just as Stoner reached him.

The man hadn't expected his next victim to fight back. He'd been reaching for the whip on his belt, but he threw up his hands to block the branch. Marc was a few seconds quicker. The limb hit Stoner on the bridge of the nose.

Blood spurted everywhere, and to Marc's total astonishment, Stoner went down.

He'd broken the man's nose. Maybe he'd also fractured his skull, because Stoner didn't move.

He'd fallen right next to Klammer. Marc stared at the two of them, breaking out in a cold sweat in spite of the heat, trembling as if he'd fall down.

He didn't want to touch Stoner, to feel for yet another pulse that wasn't there. He could detect no breathing, no rise and fall of the chest. Breathing so heavily that he thought he would pass out, Marc studied the disaster scene. It had happened even though he had vowed to himself to stay out of trouble until Dad came to get him.

I didn't mean to kill him. I just couldn't stand here and let him kill me.

Off to the side, Rat whimpered.

Marc spun, rushing to him, picking up the pup. Rat, at least, was alive.

He tried to think, to plan, to figure out what they might do to him if he went back to camp and confessed what had happened.

But the only thing that ran through his mind was panic. He'd killed Stoner. There were no witnesses. They'd shut him up in a place like this for the rest of his life. Even if they tried him in a juvenile court, they could lock him up until he was eighteen. Not even Dad would be able to rescue him.

The only coherent idea his mind could handle was to run.

"Yreka coming up," Jenny said cheerfully, jerking him out of his morbid thoughts. "I have to turn on the other side, so I'll let you off in town. There's a Pacific Pride fuel stop on the side street. It's a card lock. Lots of trucks stop there. You'll probably get a ride in no time."

Marc thanked her and got out at the station, which was empty and fairly isolated. No one was in attendance; the truckers stuck their member cards into a machine to get their fuel.

Already the temperature was dropping. How could it have been so hot just a few hours ago, hot enough to kill Klammer, and now be chilly enough that he was shaking with the cold? Or were the day's events simply too gruesome for him to deal with?

He was carrying Rat, and when he put him down, the dog immediately sniffed out a spot in which to piddle. Marc found a hose that produced a stream of tepid water that tasted of plastic. Rat drank it eagerly, Marc with less enthusiasm, but at least it was wet. He felt he should save what was in his bottles.

He decided that this was as good a time as any to eat the discarded hamburger he'd salvaged. He sat down against the dispenser that held oilcans and got it out, dividing it with Rat. He decided that since Rat was a lot smaller, he could have the lesser half of it. Rat's was gone in a gulp, leaving him watching Marc's chewing.

An eighteen-wheeler pulled in at the forward pumps. The logo said ACE JOHANSON, PORTLAND, OR. Marc watched as the driver inserted his card in the machine, then started pumping diesel. Should he approach him, or not? Portland was in the right direction, several hundred miles closer to Seattle.

Lifting Rat again, to make sure the driver knew the dog was part of the package, Marc walked across the lot.

The driver was middle-aged, bald, with a potbelly. He looked up when Marc said, "Hi."

"Hi," the driver said. He was chewing bubble gum and needed a shave.

"Any chance I could get a ride into Portland?" His heart must be about worn out now, with all the stress it had been through, he thought.

"Could," the driver said. "Only I just came from there. I'm headed for L.A."

"Oh." Disappointment was sour in his throat. "Okay, thanks anyway."

"You're young to be hitchhiking," the driver said.

"Yeah." The lie came readily to his tongue this time. "Somebody stole my bus ticket money."

The man's eyes narrowed. "You got any money left for food?"

"No," Marc said honestly.

"I usually eat in restaurants," the driver said, "so I'm not carrying much. I could let you have some junk food if you're hungry."

The hamburger hadn't even begun to fill him up. "Junk food would be great," Marc said.

"Let's see what I got left," the man muttered, leaving the hose in the tank opening and reaching up inside the cab. "A bag of corn chips, two Mars bars, an orange, and, uh—a burrito. It's cold."

"Cold's okay." It all sounded wonderful, if only his stomach would settle down and he could be sure nothing would come back up.

He shared the burrito with Rat after the trucker had gone. This time guilt made him share evenly.

Four more trucks pulled in over the next half hour. Two of them were heading south. A third was having some kind of mechanical problem and the driver called in to request a mechanic. The fourth cut Marc off with a "Sorry" before he had even finished making his request.

He was downright cold by now. He scrunched down between the oil dispenser and a Coke machine, out of the breeze, and held Rat on his lap, glad of his warmth.

What could Dad do, even when he reached him? Everybody knew he'd gone out to check on Klammer, and they probably all knew Stoner had followed him there. Had Privett gone back and reported anything, or just chickened out and returned to the barracks and told nobody anything? How long would it have been before any of the staff checked on Stoner?

Rat whined and licked at his chin. At least Rat hadn't been killed though. It wouldn't have surprised him if the dog had suffered some broken ribs, the way Stoner had kicked him. For a moment he reflected that Stoner had deserved that heavy limb in the face, and then rationality set in. As he'd heard repeatedly in those anger management classes, Marc remembered there were better ways to handle anger than killing somebody, or even beating them up.

Of course, he hadn't intended to kill Stoner, just to stop him, but how much weight would that carry? As Quincy had told them, if you didn't work your problems out somehow without violence, you were going to wind up behind bars. The public would only tolerate so much antisocial behavior, and then they locked you up. No matter how good your reason was for whatever you'd done.

He was half-dozing, despite the chill, and didn't even notice the truck pulling in.

The voice startled him wide awake.

The driver came toward him, walking purposefully.

"Hey!" he said. Behind him was a white and blue eighteen-wheeler. "Are you Hank Solie's kid?"

And Marc didn't know if he'd been caught, or rescued.

17

"You know my dad?" Marc asked, scrambling to his feet.

"He's my dispatcher. They sent out the order—watch out for a fourteen-year-old, ran away from some camp. You Marc Solie?"

"Yeah. Is my dad okay?"

"Yeah, guess he is now. He's back at work, anyway." The driver was thirtyish, blond, well-built, and dressed in jeans and a black T-shirt with a white truck on it, stenciled with scarlet flames to indicate its speed. "If I find you, I'm supposed to bring you in."

Relief flooded over him, leaving Marc limp. "All right! My dad's been off work? How come?"

"Didn't hear the details. I think he was in some kind of accident. Come on, climb in." He eyed Rat. "Nobody told me about a dog."

"He's mine," Marc said quickly. "He goes with me."

"Whatever. I'll call in and let them know we're coming."

"How long will it take to get to Seattle?" Marc asked, boosting Rat ahead of him into the cab.

"Nine or ten hours, with two of us driving. Ted's in the sleeper," the driver said, and moved toward the front of the island to insert his credit card.

It was a long way up into the truck. "Was Dad badly hurt in the accident?"

"Don't know any details. Only know he was in the hospital."

He slammed the door, and Marc felt that at last he could relax a little. On his lap, Rat was already asleep, his belly full of burrito and corn chips.

When they stopped in Ashland, the trucker, whose name was Jimmy, woke up his partner and they all went into the truck stop restaurant. They bought steak dinners, including one for Marc. The meal was enormous, with thick-cut fries and buttered corn and salad, hot biscuits and berry pie. After Marc had eaten his fill, there was plenty left over for Rat when they went back to the truck.

"Why don't you crawl in the sleeper with me," Jimmy suggested. "Let Ted drive for a few hours." Marc was glad to comply.

He woke several times, briefly, as the big truck roared through the night, up I-5 through Oregon, taking 205 around Portland, and then down the homestretch to Seattle.

He'd hoped to get in direct touch with his father, but Jimmy said all he could do was communicate, by CB, with the office. Jimmy was told that Hank Solie had gone home, but nobody answered when they tried the phone there. This seemed peculiar, since he lived with his mother and Grandma seldom went anywhere.

Dad had known he'd run away from Camp Heritage. Did that mean he knew about Stoner and Klammer, too? He must, Marc figured. He was really grateful that it was

K & M drivers who'd picked him up, not the cops.

No doubt the police wouldn't be far behind, though. He tried not to think about it. Tried to rest. Tried not to worry.

Once, as he'd crawled back into the front seat around dawn when Ted and Jimmy again traded places, a Washington State Patrol screamed past them, doing eighty or more, lights and sirens clearing the way.

"Somebody's in trouble," Jimmy commented, unconcerned. Marc felt his heart in his throat for a few minutes, until they came upon a scene in which half a dozen emergency vehicles surrounded a three-car pile-up.

Not me. Not yet. But he knew it would be soon. *Please, let Dad be with me before that happens.* He felt sheepish when he realized he'd been close to praying there, without having intended to.

"Have to unload our cargo before we can pull the truck into the yard," Jimmy said. "Maybe we better try to let your dad know we're almost there."

It washed over him again, the wave of panic. The stress, the dread, the hope, the rapid heartbeat. Marc stiffened enough that Rat stirred on his lap.

Jimmy thumbed the mike. "Jimmy, calling dispatcher," he said.

The voice was familiar, and so dear. Marc's palms were damp, same as his eyes.

"Solie here," Dad said.

"Solie, got your kid. Picked him up in Yreka. I'll have him there within the hour. Have to unload on the waterfront first."

"Ten-four," Dad said. And then, "I'll come and get

him. Tell him to hang in there, I'll be there in twenty minutes. Pier twelve, right?"

"Ten-four," Jimmy confirmed.

He'd made it. He was within Dad's reach. Now all he had to worry about was the police, but at least he wouldn't be facing them alone.

First Dad hugged him, then he read him the riot act.

"I couldn't believe what they were telling me about my son."

"I didn't know what to do," Marc said, an understatement if there ever was one.

"Just keep praying," Dad said, "through all the bad things, and wait for help, I guess. Thank God you're okay."

Marc squirmed a little. "I didn't do much praying, Dad. In fact, I hardly did any."

"Well, I did. All the time I couldn't talk to you, and then when your mother called yesterday—"

"Mom called you?" Marc was astonished.

"That Captain Jasper at Camp Heritage called her and said you'd run away. So she called me, just the way she should have done."

Involuntarily, Marc suspended his breathing. "What did he say?"

"That you'd run away. They'd notified the police, thinking you might be heading for home in Eureka, but your mother didn't think you'd go back to her. She thought you'd try to get to me."

"Did—did they say anything about Sergeant Stoner?"

Dad regarded him soberly. "You attacked him, they said." His eyes begged for a denial that Marc couldn't provide.

"He kicked Rat, and I thought he'd killed him. And he'd already staked Klammer out in the sun, for hours, and he was . . . dead when I found him. And I thought Stoner was going to kill me, too. . . ." Marc trailed off, then had to ask the question. "He . . . he's dead too, isn't he?"

"No, actually he's just in the hospital with a fractured skull and a broken nose," Dad said. "They said his condition was 'serious.'"

Something broke, warm and wet and spreading, inside of him. "I didn't kill him?"

"No, but you might have. It's pretty serious, Marc, to hurt somebody that bad."

Marc ran his tongue over dry lips. "Is he going to die?"

"They don't know yet, but they usually say 'critical' rather than 'serious' if he's that bad. Your mother understood that you had anger management classes—"

"None of the things they wanted us to do instead of violence could have worked right then," Marc said earnestly. "There was nobody to talk to, nothing to do but defend myself. I really thought he was going to kill me, Dad! What else could I have done?"

"I don't know. Probably a judge and a jury will have to decide whether what you did was justified or not. I've called a lawyer. We have an appointment late this afternoon, after I get off work."

A judge and a jury. The words were chilling. "Am—am I going to have to go to jail?"

"Well, if the authorities had caught up with you while you were still in California, you might have been held. Since you made it to Washington State, there'll be some legal wrangling. I'm hoping this lawyer can keep you in my custody until there's a hearing. I think they'll have to extradite you to California, and that'll give us a little time to figure out what's best to do."

"Isn't it legal to protect yourself? Isn't that self-defense?"

"Yes. But they may decide this Stoner fellow didn't intend to kill you, in which case your attack wasn't justifiable."

"Klammer was already dead, and it was Stoner's fault. So I don't think I was out of line to be afraid of him. There was nobody there to see it. No witness." Marc was as dry as he'd been in the hottest part of the day at Camp Heritage. "What . . . what'll happen if Stoner dies?"

"They might charge you with manslaughter. Under the circumstances, I doubt if the charge would be murder. We'll have a better idea after we talk to the lawyer. Try not to worry about it, son. We're going to do the best we can to work this out."

So the nightmare wasn't over. Marc wondered if it ever would be. Could he ever again experience dry heat and drenching sweat and the smell of pines and cedars and spruce trees, ever hear the whisper of a breeze in the tops of the trees, without remembering the lifeless body of Klammer crumpled in the red dirt, and feeling sick to his stomach?

He'd swallowed hard so many times his throat was sore. "I tried to get in touch with you, Dad," he said. "We didn't have any e-mail, and when I called the house nobody answered."

Dad reached out again and put an arm around him, walking him to the car while Jimmy's truck was being unloaded behind them. "I'm sorry about that, Marc. I never dreamed you were going through anything like this. My computer fried, and I still don't have a replacement, though I've got one ordered. It was one thing after another, and I thought you'd be okay until I got through everything else that was falling apart around me."

"Like what?" Marc asked, thankful for the comfort of that heavy arm across his shoulders.

"Well, first it was Ma. Your grandmother started having chest pain, angina, and when we took her into the emergency room, they had to do a lot of tests to figure out where the blockages were. Then they decided she'd be better off with bypass surgery, only she was stubborn about that, didn't want it. They put her on medication, which helped some, but eventually they persuaded her to have two stents put it."

"What's a stent?" Marc wanted to know.

"Well, you know that the chest pain is because there is a narrowing or a blockage in an artery, that makes your heart pump harder to push the blood through. Sometimes they do surgery and take a vein from somewhere else to build a bypass around the clogged area. Sometimes they can put in what they call a stent, right where the blockage is, and hold it open. So that's what they did."

"And is she okay now?"

"She's better. But she's still on medication, and couldn't go home right away, couldn't manage by herself. So she's having rehabilitation in a nursing facility, and when you tried to call me at her house I was either over there with her or in the hospital myself." He looked a little sheepish at this admission.

"Jimmy said you were in an accident."

"Got broadsided. I was on the way to the rest home and a drunk ran a stop sign. Luckily he hit the passenger side—mangled my car, but didn't injure me too seriously. I was in the hospital three days before they decided it was safe to turn me loose."

"But you're okay now?"

"Okay now. When I called down at the house, your mom said you were off at camp somewhere. I asked how come, since school wasn't even out for the summer, and she said somebody was at the door and she'd explain later. Only she never did, until she called late yesterday and admitted you were at a wilderness camp." Indignation etched his face. "I couldn't believe it!"

"Neither could I. Floyd talked her into it."

"I'm going to have to hear why she allowed anything like this to happen without consulting me. I'm still your father, and this was a pretty drastic decision to make."

So Marc explained the things that had happened to

infuriate Floyd. "I don't like him, Dad, and he doesn't like me. I think she's going to marry him. Did she say she was going to marry him?"

"No. She never mentioned Floyd to me."

"If she does marry him, am I going to have to live with them? With him and his daughters?"

"I've been working toward having you come and live with me. I don't know if that would mean a court battle over custody or not. I hate to put your mother through something like that—she was adamant when we separated that she wanted to retain custody. But that hasn't worked out very well."

"No," Marc agreed, with a heartfelt sigh.

"Gram and I talked about it, whether I should stay on in her house and bring you up from California, or get a place of our own. It's kind of up in the air right now. Ma sure isn't in any shape to keep house for us. You're going to have to pitch in and help me with the cooking and cleaning, whatever needs to be done. I think Ma's going to be able to come back home after rehab, but she may need a live-in caregiver. We don't know yet."

Remembering all the adjustments he'd been called upon to make at Camp Heritage, Marc assured his dad that they would be able to manage, no matter what he had to do. If he was allowed to stay with him, that was.

The meeting with the lawyer, whose name was Radner, was sobering.

"You were there because of behavioral problems," the man said. He was a little older than Marc's dad, going gray, trim, and serious in manner. "And then you attacked one of the camp instructors with a club and seriously injured him."

Marc wondered if he'd ever get past the point where his mouth was so dry his tongue stuck to the roof of it. "Yes, sir. But he'd just killed another cadet. All of us kids knew how dangerous it was to leave him out there in the hot sun, without even a hat or a water bottle. And Stoner knew it too. He was always on everybody to wear hats and drink enough so we didn't get dehydrated. He told us it was a disciplinary matter if we got dehydrated, because we knew how extreme sunstroke could be."

If he was winning the man over to his point of view, it wasn't obvious. Mr. Radner sat behind his big desk with his hands tented before him, not changing expression.

Desperation enveloped him as Marc sought to make the man understand. "Klammer is dead, right?"

"Oh, yes. He's dead." Radner hesitated, then contributed to their knowledge. "The camp is being closed down. The boys are being sent to other facilities."

"Jail?" Marc asked, suddenly remembering them all: Coleman and Privett and McCloud and all the others. Castoffs. Boys nobody wanted. Boys who had been abused, mistreated, brutalized. Boys who could not behave in a socially acceptable way. "Where will they all go? Will any of them go home?"

But their homes were not safe places either. Klammer's grandmother peddled drugs—but then Marc remembered that Klammer was dead; he wouldn't need to go home.

"I have no information about that," Radner stated.

"Most of them will probably end up in some sort of juvenile detention center. One way or another, each of them has crossed the line. They can't just be forgiven and turned loose."

And, by unspoken suggestion, neither could Marc.

He glanced at his father, and saw nothing encouraging in Hank Solie's face. Dad, Marc realized, was afraid for him. The boy felt as if worms were crawling through him, determined to destroy him.

Radner rocked back in his chair, fixing a cold blue gaze on Marc. "Tell me exactly what happened that last day at camp."

So Marc told him. In great detail, several times, with Radner asking all sorts of questions. By the time the man was satisfied, Marc was limp and half-sick to his stomach. And from the expression on his dad's face, Marc thought he was feeling much the same way.

"Can you keep him out of police custody?" Hank Solie asked, his voice husky.

"For a few days, at least. They're going to want him back in California for questioning."

"I can go with him, right?"

"Well, I'll be there for the initial questioning, and it'll undoubtedly go to a grand jury. They'll determine what charges will be brought. A lot will depend on what happens to this Sergeant Stoner. If he dies, there may be a manslaughter charge."

"But you'll argue for self-defense, right?" Hank asked. Marc noticed that his father's knuckles were white on the arm of his chair.

For the first time Radner smiled, transforming his face. "Oh, you bet. I'll be fighting any charges with everything I've got." The smile vanished as if it had never been, the steely gaze settling on Marc. "Don't get overconfident. There are hurdles to get past. But I think we've got a good chance to make a grand jury listen to reason. The fact that your father didn't know you were being sent to that place, and that the other boy died, may give us some leverage. The camp's been closed, so they won't send you back there, and without your father's permission it's unlikely they would put you in another such place. Unless they vote to bring you to trial on either murder or manslaughter charges."

The words hung in the air between them. Marc wiped his palms on his pant legs.

Chasms loomed before him. His entire future was at risk, all because of some very minor and stupid things. Floyd had wanted him out of the way, and it was excruciatingly painful to know that his mother had gone along with it.

"I'll be in touch," Radner said, "when I get the papers from California." He stood up, and it was over, for now.

But Marc knew that it would never really be over, no matter what happened to Stoner or what the grand jury decided.

Klammer would still be dead, and whether Stoner lived or died, Marc would be the one responsible for his injuries.

For the rest of his life, he'd be facing the consequences of what had happened at Camp Heritage.

18

The California authorities were irate because Marc had fled the state.

Radner was unperturbed about what anyone else thought. There were local detectives who came to the house and talked to Marc and his father, then agreed to meet later in Radner's office after the lawyer advised them against talking outside his presence.

There were stalling actions Radner could take to keep Marc in Washington State—papers to be filed and refiled; arguments made. All perfectly legitimate, the lawyer assured them. All designed to provide him with thinking and working time.

In a way Marc was gratified by each step that kept the California authorities at bay a little. In another way, he knew that sooner or later they would have to be faced, and a part of him wished they could do it and get the worst of matters behind him.

Gram was still in rehab, at the rest home. Marc and Hank did their own cooking, cleaned up the kitchen and the bathroom, ran the vacuum through the rest of Gram's house.

"She always kept it tidy, so we want it to be that way when she comes home," Dad said.

Marc went beyond what Dad suggested he do. It

was easy, compared to being at Camp Heritage.

It was almost the end of the school year, and nobody suggested Marc return to classes in Seattle. He didn't think he could have learned or retained a thing anyway.

He had nightmares. Twice he made enough noise that Dad came in and woke him up. He sat on the edge of his son's bed and they talked a while, until Marc calmed down enough to try to go back to sleep.

"I keep seeing Klammer, lying there with his face in the dirt. He was a jerk, a real troublemaker, but he didn't deserve to die that way. I keep remembering that he was warm when I touched him, and I thought I'd got there in time, that he was still alive, only he wasn't. It didn't seem right that he was so warm but was actually dead."

Dad didn't say anything, just laid a big hand over his son's.

"And Stoner—I really thought he was going to kill me, Dad. He'd already left Klammer to die, and I thought he'd kicked Rat hard enough to kill him, and that I was next. I saw the heavy tree limb and picked it up, because it looked like Stoner was going for his whip. I knew what he could do with that whip; I never saw him use it on a person, but he could cut leaves off trees, knock cans off fence posts, and I thought—"

Dad's hand tightened.

"I swung it as hard as I could. Maybe I wasn't really thinking, I was so scared of what he was going to do, but I knew I'd only get one chance at stopping him. I got stronger, you know, chopping all that wood, and I put every muscle I had into it."

He could see it all again, was living through it again. "The blood spurted out of his nose and his mouth, and it got on my hands, and he went down. I was so sure he was dead, but I couldn't make myself touch him to be sure. I didn't dare go back to camp and tell anybody—all I could think of was to get to you."

Dad sat for a minute, not speaking. When he finally stood up he looked down at Rat, curled at the bottom of the bed against Marc's feet. "I don't know what Gram's going to say about a dog in her sheets." He, too, found it difficult to talk about the important stuff.

"He keeps me company," Marc said. "Dad, do you think I should call Mom? Or have you talked to her?"

"You can call her anytime you like." He cleared his throat. "I talked to her after we saw Radner for the first time. She's really upset about what's happened. She feels guilty."

Marc didn't know how to respond to that. He felt she *should* feel guilty. "She doesn't . . . hate me, does she?"

"No. She knows it wasn't all your fault, Marc. Try to get some sleep."

Not all his fault. But partly, then. He'd partly brought it on himself, though if he'd been dealing solely with Mom and not Floyd, it would never have gone so far. Mom by herself would never have sent him to Camp Heritage. She probably hadn't even known there were such places.

It was his own turn to clear his throat. "I wonder if Floyd asked for a refund on what he paid to send me there."

Dad made a small sound, deep in his throat. "Ah . . . she said she isn't seeing Floyd anymore. So she wouldn't know."

Marc's heart leaped in his first positive feeling in some time. "I'm glad. He . . . wasn't good for her."

"No," Dad agreed.

"She hadn't given up Mallory's things yet."

"No," Dad repeated.

"Do you think—will she ever get better? Back to the way she used to be? If she doesn't get over Mallory?"

"I don't know, son. I just keep praying this will all work out, but I don't know if it will ever be the same as it used to be."

Dad's prayers *had* been answered, at least about Marc's reaching him.

Maybe it was worth trying again himself. Maybe with Floyd out of the picture, Mom and Dad could consider getting back together.

He didn't dare voice that hope. But in the dark, after Dad had gone back to bed, he let the tears seep out of his eyes and prayed that God would make everything all right.

It would be a miracle if He did. But Marc knew that nothing was impossible to an all-powerful God, so he let his hopes build that it would happen.

Marc hadn't gotten up the nerve to call his mother yet. And he thought about the other cadets at Camp Heritage a lot, and worried about them. Where had they been taken? Did Coleman ever get back to his girlfriend? Would he get to marry her and be a father?

Would any of them have to return to a home with an abusive father and a drug-dealing grandma? Would Privett be allowed to rejoin his father and the new family, and be able to stop doing hateful things to his stepsisters? Would anyone else take over the job of teaching McCloud to read, so he could do better in school and eventually get a job and support himself?

What would happen to Stoner if he recovered fully? Surely he, too, would be facing at least manslaughter charges. Now that he was somewhat calmed down, Marc couldn't believe that the man had actually intended to murder Klammer, but he was responsible for the welfare of the boys under his authority. He should have known how dangerous it was to leave a cadet in that terrible heat without water. He had to have been aware of that, or why else would he have been so insistent on hats and water?

Marc was alone all day in the house, with only Rat for company. He got a regular leash and collar and walked him a lot. He went to visit Grandma. She hadn't been told about the mess at Camp Heritage, which was a relief because he didn't have to talk about it or see her distress over it. He and Dad had the house shining clean and a macaroni casserole—with three kinds of cheese—ready when she finally came home.

She didn't ask him a lot of questions, just seemed glad to see him and Dad and be home. She took to Rat right away when he licked at her hand and begged to be put on her lap. She didn't come into Marc's bedroom, so she didn't even notice that Rat slept on his bed.

And then one day Dad came in smiling and said, "News."

"Good?" Marc demanded, his recently calmed-down heart suddenly pounding again.

"Well, I think so. We're finally going to face the law in California and get some things settled."

The butterflies in his stomach threatened to erupt. "That's good?"

"It means it won't be hanging over us any longer. One way or the other, we'll know where we stand. Radner's going down with us; we won't have to face that grand jury by ourselves. If we're lucky, they'll listen to him and they won't indict you at all."

"But what if they *do*?" He struggled not to crumple, the way he felt like doing.

"Then we'll face that, too. In the meantime, we have to have faith and keep on praying. One of our prayers has been answered, anyway." Dad's smile widened.

"What?" Marc asked, squeezing Rat so hard the dog squeaked a protest.

"Radner just heard: Sergeant Stoner is out of the coma, out of intensive care. He's going to live, and he's going to be charged with that Klammer kid's death."

Air whooshed out of Marc's lungs. "No murder charge against me! Right?"

"Right. The fact that he's going to be held responsible for what happened to Klammer means there's less likelihood they'll be out to nail *you*." Dad hesitated, then added, "That's my interpretation; Radner didn't tell me that. But we leave in the morning for California. So pack a week's worth of stuff, okay?"

Tomorrow. California. A grand jury. *Terrifying*.

But Stoner was going to live, and Marc hoped the man would tell the truth about what had happened—maybe even admit what his intentions toward Marc had been.

Nothing had happened yet to indicate his folks might get back together. Maybe they never would, but it didn't hurt to hope, did it?

And maybe it wouldn't hurt to pray a little either. For the other cadets, for whatever was happening to them. For his own family. For a reasonable grand jury.

Marc stared at his dad through misty eyes. "I'll go pack now," he said. And he swelled with pride and trust as Dad wrapped him in a bear hug so hard it hurt.

He thought maybe there was moisture in Dad's eyes as well. And maybe the reserved Radner really cared too.

The nightmare might not be over, but it was beginning to fade.

Marc paused in the doorway, swallowing audibly. "Maybe—do you think if I called and talked to Mom, that she'd—meet us there?"

He thought he saw the same emotion in Dad's eyes as there must have been in his own.

"I don't know, son. But it won't hurt to ask."

Miracles. He wanted miracles.

They were hard to come by, but it wouldn't hurt to ask.